ADVENTURE STORIES FOR
SIX YEAR OLDS

Helen Paiba is known as one of the most committed, knowledgeable and acclaimed children's booksellers in Britain. For more than twenty years she owned and ran the Children's Bookshop in Muswell Hill, London, which under her guidance gained a superb reputation for its range of children's books and for the advice available to its customers.

Helen was involved with the Booksellers Association for many years and served on both its Children's Bookselling Group and the Trade Practices Committee. In 1995 she was given honorary life membership of the Booksellers Association of Great Britain and Ireland in recognition of her outstanding services to the association and to the book trade. In the same year the Children's Book Circle (sponsored by Books for Children) honoured her with the Eleanor Farjeon Award, given for distinguished service to the world of children's books.

She retired in 1995 and now lives in London.

Adventure
STORIES
for Six Year Olds

COMPILED BY HELEN PAIBA

ILLUSTRATED BY BEN CORT

MACMILLAN
CHILDREN'S BOOKS

For Jade with love HP

First published 2000 by Macmillan Children's Books
a division of Macmillan Publishers Limited
20 New Wharf Road, London N1 9RR
Basingstoke and Oxford
www.panmacmillan.com

Associated companies throughout the world

ISBN 0 330 39138 0

7 9 8

A CIP catalogue record for this book is available from
the British Library.

Typeset by SX Composing DTP, Rayleigh, Essex
Printed and bound in India by
Replika Press Pvt. Ltd.

Contents

The Witch and the Little Village Bus

Margaret Stuart Barry

Simon was late for school. So that was how he came to jump on the village bus. And that was how he happened to meet Ginny the witch. He had sat down next to her before he had properly noticed her.

She was a very ugly old witch. She had a pale green face, tiny red eyes like hot cinders, a spot on the end of her long nose, and grey hair which reached down to her knees. Simon was pleased. He liked witches. He hoped she was going to be a really wicked old witch like the ones he had read about.

"What have you got in your bag?" he asked her.

"In my bag? – My magic wand, of course, my Post Office Savings Book, and my knitting."

"Oh," said Simon.

He was a little disappointed. He had hoped that the witch would have had a black toad, or at least a couple of dead spiders. They were passing the school gates, but

2

Simon was too interested to notice.

"Fares please," said the conductor. Simon paid his fare.

"Fares," said the conductor to the witch.

"You forgot to say 'please'," reminded Ginny the witch.

"Why should I say 'please' to an old witch like you," said the conductor, rudely.

"Because it's manners," replied the witch.

"Fares!" snapped the conductor.

"If you do not say 'please', I shall change your silly old bus into something else."

The conductor was now very

cross. "Shan't," he said.

At that, the witch opened her handbag and started to search for her wand. As soon as she found it, she changed the bus into a fast express train.

"Wheeeeeee!" went the fast express train. It shot down the

village street, through the red
lights, and out on to the motorway.
On the motorway was a big sign
which said – LONDON 50 MILES.

"Hey!" shouted Farmer Spud.
"I do not want to go to London.
I want to go to Little Hampton
to buy a pig."

"Hey!" shouted Mrs Gummidge.
"I do not want to go to London
either. I want to go to Little
Hampton to buy some shoelaces."

"Hey!" said the bus driver. "I do
not know how to drive this thing.
It is much too fast."

Ginny the witch said nothing.
She took her knitting out of her
bag and began to knit, very fast.

5

Simon was delighted.

It was not very long before the roaring train reached London. There were cars and buses everywhere. The train was bumping into them one after another.

"This is terrible!" said the conductor. "Stop, stop it!"

"I will if you say 'please'. Otherwise I shall change your silly old train into something else."

"I will not say 'please' to a witch," shouted the rude conductor.

"Suit yourself," said Ginny. She put away her knitting, searched again for her wand, and changed

6

the train into a green caterpillar.

"Help!" cried Farmer Spud, falling off.

"Help!" cried Mrs Gummidge, falling off also.

"Help! Help!" cried the conductor and the bus driver.

The caterpillar was far too slippery to ride on. It was also much too small. The passengers were obliged to walk alongside it.

"This is ridiculous!" complained Farmer Spud. "I have never been on a bus like this in the whole of my life."

"You are not on it, man, are you!" snapped Mrs Gummidge, irritably.

7

"Watch it!" cried the bus driver.
"It's going down that grid!"

Laughing, Simon rescued the
little caterpillar and set it on its
way again. It was actually a great
deal of trouble and bother
watching the caterpillar. First it
went this way, and then the other.
It did not seem to have any clear
idea where it wanted to go. The
bus driver was extremely worried
about it. He had to get his bus
back to the Depot by six o'clock.
It was already half past four.
Suddenly a big policeman
stepped into the road to direct
the traffic.

"Watch out!" gasped the bus

driver. "You're stepping on our bus!"

The big London policeman looked around in all directions. He could not see a bus. He could see only a bus driver, a conductor, a farmer, an old woman, a small boy, and a very ugly witch.

"I'm busy," he said. "Mind out."

"This is terrible," moaned the bus driver. "For goodness sake, say 'please' to the old witch."

"I cannot possibly," said the conductor. "I never say 'please' to witches."

"Suit yourself," said Ginny. She had almost finished her knitting.

It was nearing the Rush Hour.

The Rush Hour is a terrible thing.
Trains and buses and cars and
people rush about everywhere in a
great hurry. They squash and push
and squeeze each other. There is
certainly no room for a caravan
drawn by six cart-horses. So this is
what the witch decided to do. She
pulled out her wand and changed
the little caterpillar into a
handsome caravan, drawn by six
cart-horses. The caravan took up a
lot more room than the caterpillar
had done. Moreover, the cart-
horses could not tell green lights
from red lights: they clattered
clumsily on. They did not
understand what the policemen

were shouting about. When cars and buses kicked them, they kicked back with a will.

"This is great!" cried Simon. "It's better than school!"

"This is monstrous!" cried the bus driver.

"My pig! My shoelaces!" cried Farmer Spud and Mrs Gummidge together, looking at the time. It was now five o'clock. They would never get back to the Depot. The six cart-horses caught sight of Hyde Park. It looked nice and green. They trotted in for a feed of grass.

"They can't do that!" exclaimed the bus driver. "There isn't time!"

11

"It's your conductor who is making us late – not my horses," said Ginny. "Anyway, I'm tired." She hung up her hat on a branch and sat down under a tree for a nap.

"She's going to sleep!" cried Farmer Spud, indignantly. He shook her, and said, "Wake up, wake up – you bad old witch."

"Go away," yawned Ginny. "I've had a hard day."

No one knew what to do – except Simon. He had run off to play with the horses. He did not mind one bit how late it was.

Then Mrs Gummidge got very cross. "Now just you listen to me, conductor," she scolded – prodding him in the tummy with her umbrella. "It is high time we went home. We have had enough of this nonsense. Mend your manners and say 'please' to that old witch at once."

"But I never say 'please' to—"

Mrs Gummidge poked her umbrella a little harder.

"Oh, very well," grumbled the conductor. He was worn out anyway. He shuffled over to Ginny.

"Fares please," he said in a sulky voice.

Ginny opened one red eye, and said, "Pardon?"

"Fares please," said the

13

conductor again.

Ginny put one finger into her ear and rubbed it very hard until it squeaked. "Pardon?" she said again.

"Fares – please." This time the conductor said it very politely.

"Now that's better!" declared the witch.

She whisked out her wand and she changed the caravan and the six cart-horses into a big jet. Everybody scrambled in as fast as they could.

"Zooooom!" went the jet – and before the bus driver, or the conductor, or the farmer, or the old woman, or the little boy had

14

time to think – they were in Little Hampton.

The shops were shut, so it was too late for Farmer Spud to buy his pig, or Mrs Gummidge her shoelaces. But it was still only one minute before six o'clock – just enough time for the witch to change the big jet plane back into the village bus.

"Thank you, Madam," said the conductor – very politely.

"You're welcome," said the witch. "Any time."

Then she went home with Simon, to explain to Simon's mother why he was home a little late for tea.

Tashi and the Genie

Anna Fienberg and Barbara Fienberg

Jack and Tashi ran up the wharf and hurtled onto the ferry. They flung themselves down on a seat outside, just as the boat chugged off.

Tashi watched the white water foam behind them. The sun was warm and gentle on their faces. Jack closed his eyes.

"What a magical day!" they heard a woman say as she brushed

past them. Jack's eyes snapped open.

"Talking of magic," he said to Tashi, "let's hear about the time you saw that genie. What did he look like? How did you meet him?"

"Well," said Tashi, taking a breath of sea air, "it was like this. One day, not long before I came to this country, I was in the shed looking for some nails. Grandmother called me, saying she wanted a few eggs. I gathered about four or five from under the hens and then looked around for a dish to put them in. I spied an old, cracked one on a top shelf, covered with a dirty piece of carpet. But

17

there was something very strange about this bowl."

"Ooh," squealed Jack. "I know, I know what was in it!"

"Yes," nodded Tashi. "When I lifted the carpet I saw a bubbling grey mist inside; soft rumbling snores were coming from it. The snores turned to a splutter when I poked it. A voice groaned, 'Oh not again! Not already!' And the mist swirled and rose up in the air. Two big sleepy eyes squinted down at me. 'And only twenty-five years and ten minutes since my last master let me go!' it said. Well, I was *very* excited."

"Who *wouldn't* be," Jack agreed.

" 'You're a genie!' I shouted.
'What if I am?' said he. 'Why
aren't you in a bottle?' I asked. 'Or
a lamp, like normal genies?' The
genie looked shifty. 'Oh, my master
went off in too much of a hurry to
put me back in my lamp. So I just
crept into this bowl, hoping for
some peace and quiet.' "

Tashi winked at Jack. "I
happened to know a lot about
genies, because my grandmother
was always telling me what to do if
I met one. So I looked him in the
eye and said, 'Now that I've found
you, don't you have to grant me
three wishes?'

"The genie groaned. 'Wishes,

wishes! People don't realise they are usually better off leaving things the way they are.' But he pulled himself up to his full height and straightened his turban. 'What is your command, master?' he bowed.

"I thought for a moment. 'I would like an enormous sack of gold.' Imagine, I could build a splendid palace, for all my family to live in.

"The genie snapped his fingers and – *TA RA* – a sack of gold lay at my feet! I ran my hands through the glittering coins and held one up. Hmm, before I build the palace, I thought, I might just run down to

21

the sweet-maker's shop."

"Good idea!" cried Jack. "You could buy a *million* sweets, to last you till you're a hundred and ten!"

"Yes, but when Second Cousin at the shop took my coin, she looked at it carefully and rubbed it on her sleeve. The gold rubbed right off. 'This coin is no good, Tashi,' she told me. 'It's only copper.'

"I stamped back to the shed and angrily shook the genie out of his dish. 'Those coins are only copper!' I shouted.

"The genie yawned. 'Really? All of them? How tragic.' He stretched. 'Maybe a few at the bottom will be gold. What I need now is a glass of tea before I do any more work.'"

"What a lousy, lazy genie!" exploded Jack.

"Yes," agreed Tashi. "And it gets worse. By the time I'd brought his tea, I'd thought of my second wish. 'What about a flying carpet?' I asked. Oh, if only I'd known. The genie looked at me doubtfully. 'Flying carpets are not my best thing,' he said. But I was firm with him, so he snapped his fingers, and there, floating at my knees, was a glittering carpet. It was the most magnificent thing I had ever seen. All smooth and polished as skin, it was patterned with hundreds of tiny peacocks, with eyes glowing like jewels.

"The carpet trembled as I climbed on. The genie showed me how to tug at the corners to steer it. And then we were off, the carpet and I, out of the shed, over the house and across the village square. All the people were amazed, as they looked up and saw me waving at them."

"I bet they were!" cried Jack. "My dad would have fainted with shock. So, did you get to see Africa? Or Spain?"

"No," Tashi frowned. "It was like this. I had just turned in the direction of Africa, in fact, when

24

the carpet suddenly dipped and bucked like a wild horse. My knees slipped right to the edge! I threw myself face down on the carpet, grabbing hold of the fringe.

"The carpet heaved up and down, and side to side, trying to throw me off. A hundred times it kicked me in the belly, but I clung on. The world was swirling around me like soup in a pot, and then I saw we were heading straight for the willow tree beside my house. I came crashing down through the branches. When I got my breath back, I marched off to find the genie.

" 'Well, you certainly aren't very

25

good at your job, are you?' I
scolded as I brushed the leaves
from my hair."

"Is that all you could say?"
yelled Jack. "I would have called
him a fumble-bumble *beetle*-brain
at the very least."

"Yes, but I still wanted my third
wish," Tashi sighed. "Oh, if only
I'd known. Well, the genie just
yawned at me and said, 'What is
your third – and last – wish,
master?'

"I thought carefully. One thing I
had often longed for was to meet
Uncle Tiki Pu, my father's
Younger Brother. He had run away
to the city while he was still a boy,

but my father had told me stories of his pranks and jokes. 'Yes, that's it!' I said. 'I would like to meet my Uncle Tiki Pu.'

"It was suddenly very quiet in the shed. The genie rose up and clicked his fingers. Nothing happened. 'You will find him in your bedroom,' said the genie, and slithered back into his bowl. I ran to my bedroom and there was my uncle, stretched out on my bed.

" 'Ah, Tashi,' he said, 'it's about time someone came to find me. My life has been very hard in the city.' Before I could say that I was sorry to hear it, and how pleased the family would be to have him back

27

home again, Uncle Tiki Pu went on. 'This bed is very hard, however.'

"I looked around the room. 'Where will *I* sleep, Uncle?'

" 'Who knows?' he answered in a bored voice. 'Get me something to eat, Tashi, a little roast duck and ginger will do. And tell your mother when she comes home that these clothes need washing.'

"He pointed to a pile of clothes beside my toy box. The lid was open and inside my box were jars of hair oil and tins of tobacco instead of my train set and kite and rock collection.

" 'Where are my things?' I cried.

" 'Oh, I threw them out the window,' he told me. 'How else could I make room for my belongings?'

"I ran outside and gathered up my toys. Two wheels had fallen off my little red train.

" 'What about *my* belongings?'

I called through the window.

" 'Don't worry about them,' replied Uncle Tiki Pu. 'You won't be living here much longer. This house is too small for all of us now that I've come back. You can have my old job in the city, Tashi. But mind you take a rug to sleep on because they don't give you any bedding there, and the stony ground is crawling with giant spiders that bite. See, I've got the wounds to prove it.'

"And he lifted his holey old singlet to show big red lumps all over his tummy, like cherry tomatoes.

" 'Do they give you food in the

city?' I could hardly bear to ask.

" 'No, there's never enough, so you have to hunt for it. That's where the spiders come in handy. If you squish them first, they're not bad in a fritter. Oh, and watch out for alligators – they swim in the drains. Well, goodbye and good luck! You'll need it, ha ha!' And he laughed a wicked laugh."

Tashi stopped for a moment, because he couldn't help shivering at the terrible memory of his uncle, and also because Jack was jumping up and down on his seat in outrage. The woman who had said "What a magical day!" was staring.

31

"I know," said Tashi. "I know, I couldn't believe it either, that a member of my family could be so evil. My head was pounding, and I ran straight to see the genie."

"How could *he* help, that old *beetle*-brain?"

"Well," said Tashi. "It was like this. I picked up his bowl and tried to wake the genie again. I shook him and begged him to get rid of Uncle Tiki Pu, but he just closed his eyes tightly and said, 'Go away, Tashi. You've had your three wishes and that's that.' Suddenly I put the bowl down and smiled. I had just had a cunning idea. I remembered another thing

32

Grandmother always told me about genies.

"I hurried back to my room and said to Uncle Tiki Pu, 'You are quite right. This house is very small and poky. How would you like to live in a palace instead?'

"Uncle Tiki Pu sat up with a bounce. 'Just what I've always wanted!' he cried. 'How did you *know*?' 'Come with me,' I told him, 'and I will show you how to do it.'

"I opened the door of the shed and led him to the genie's bowl. Uncle let out a howl of joy when he saw what was curled up inside, but when the genie rose into the air, his eyes weren't sleepy any more. They were bright and sly.

" 'I am your new master, so listen carefully, Genie,' Uncle Tiki Pu began. 'For my first wish—'

"The genie interrupted him. 'There will be no wishes for you, my friend. You really should have been more careful. Don't you know that every seventh time a genie is disturbed, *he* becomes the master, and the one who wakes him must be the slave?' He glided over and arranged himself on Uncle Tiki Pu's shoulders. 'Take me to the city,' he commanded, 'and be quick about it.'

"Uncle Tiki Pu's face was bulging with rage and his knees

34

sagged, but he staggered out of the shed with his load. As he sailed past, the genie turned and gave me a big wink.

" 'Look out for alligators!' I called."

Jack was quiet for a moment, thinking. He watched people stand up and stretch as the ferry slowed, nearing the city.

"I hope nothing with teeth lives in *our* drains," he said. "Well, Tashi, that's amazing! Did you really fly on a magic carpet?"

For an answer, Tashi opened the top buttons of his jacket, showing Jack the gold coin hanging on a cord around his neck. "How else would I have this?" he said.

And the two boys stepped off the ferry and strolled over to the ice cream stand at the end of the wharf.

Hospital Fish

David Henry Wilson

The entrance to the hospital was a big glass door, which suddenly split into two. Through the middle came Mummy, wheeling Christopher and Jennifer in their pushchair, and Jeremy James, who was holding his left wrist in his right hand. They all went across a large room to a sort of counter where a grey-haired lady sat writing in a book.

"Hello," said the grey-haired lady, looking up.

"Hello," said Mummy, looking down.

"What lovely children!" said the grey-haired lady.

Jeremy James wasn't feeling lovely. He was feeling painful – or to be more precise, his left wrist was feeling painful. He'd fallen off his tricycle and, as Daddy was away trying to find London, Mummy had brought him to the Accident Centre.

"This is the patient," said Mummy, and the lady looked down at Jeremy James.

"Oh dear," she said. "And what

have you done, young man?"

The young man told her what he'd done, so she took down the details and asked Mummy to wait while she told the doctor.

Mummy, Jeremy James and the twins sat down near an elderly man with bristles and an elderly woman with a stick.

"Injured yerself, 'ave yer?" asked the man.

"Yes," said Jeremy James. "I've hurt my wrist. I fell off my tricycle."

The man said that his wife had hurt her ankle.

"Did she fall off her tricycle as well?" asked Jeremy James.

"No, she ain't learned ter drive," said the man. "She caught 'er foot in the carpet."

Jeremy James said he'd caught fish in the river and flu from liquorice allsorts, but he'd never caught a foot in a carpet.

"What did she catch it with?" he asked.

" 'er leg," said the man.

Just then a young, rosy-cheeked lady in a blue uniform came across, and Jeremy James had to go with her to see the doctor.

The doctor had a white coat, thinning red hair, twinkling blue eyes, and a painful way of waggling Jeremy James's left wrist.

"Does that hurt?" he asked.

"Owowow!" said Jeremy James.

"That sounds like yes," said the doctor. "Let's get it X-rayed, shall we?"

"What's an eggs-ray?" asked Jeremy James.

The doctor explained that it was a picture which showed if your bone was broken. Now Jeremy James had seen broken toys and broken vases and all the things Daddy broke when he was doing repairs, and so he told the doctor that his wrist wasn't broken. The doctor was a little surprised.

"How do you know?" he asked.

"Because if it was," said Jeremy

James, "my hand would have fallen off."

Nevertheless, the rosy nurse took Jeremy James along a corridor, round a bend, along another corridor, through some glass doors, and down a passage. He saw lots of doors and windows, a wheelchair here, a trolley there, a man on crutches, a woman in a dressing-gown, a man in a white coat, and a very interesting fish tank with fish and bubbles and bits of green. He would have liked to have a closer look at the fish tank, but the nurse was hurrying along, and so he hurried along with her.

When they came to the X-ray
department, the nurse handed him
over to another young lady with
glasses and a tightly tied pigtail.

"Yes, I'll look after him," said the
pigtailed lady. "Just wait here,
Jeremy James, and I'll come for
you as soon as I'm ready."

She disappeared into a dark

43

room, and closed the door. Jeremy James sat on a red chair, and looked around. There were three other chairs, all empty, a little table with some old magazines, and nothing and nobody else.

Jeremy James's thoughts turned to the fish tank. Now *that* would be interesting. He wouldn't mind waiting for the pigtailed lady at the fish tank, because then he'd have something to look at. Fish, for instance. And after all, the pigtailed lady had said she'd come for him when she was ready, and it wouldn't make any difference to her if he was sitting in a red chair or standing beside a fish tank.

Jeremy James gently slid off the chair, taking care not to bump his damaged wrist, and set off up the passage towards the glass doors. On the other side of these were several corridors that went in different directions, but he was pretty sure that the fish tank was along *that* corridor, and so *that* was the corridor he took.

The fish tank wasn't along *that* corridor. There were doors, windows, and a long-haired young man who said hello, a bald-headed man who didn't say hello, and a fat lady with a thin broom.

Maybe the fish tank was along *this* corridor . . . No, there didn't seem to be anything at all along *this* corridor . . . In fact *this* corridor just led to another corridor, but at least there was someone in the other corridor – a black lady pushing a trolley of tea and sandwiches.

"Excuse me," said Jeremy James.

"Hello, dear," said the black lady.

"Can you tell me the way to the fish tank?"

"Fish tank?" exclaimed the lady. "You won't find no fish tank here, dear, this is a hospital."

"There *is* a fish tank, because I've seen it!" said Jeremy James.

"Then it must be in the kitchen," said the lady. "Just go down the

corridor, and turn to the right.
That way . . ."

She pointed.

"Thank you!" said Jeremy James.

"Here," she said. "Have a piece o'
fruit cake."

Jeremy James thanked her even
more, and with fruit cake in hand
and mouth set off down the
corridor. The black lady watched
him go, shook her head, and
pushed her trolley through a
swing door, muttering, "Fish tank.
I never seen no fish tank. I thought
they got their fish from the
fishmonger."

The kitchen was full of pots and
pans and big ovens and steam and

people in white coats and hats.

"Hullo there!" said a red-faced, black-moustached, bushy-browed man. "Enjoying our fruit cake?"

"Yes, thank you," said Jeremy James.

"Then have another piece."

Jeremy James didn't say no.

"Visiting somebody, are you?"

"No," said Jeremy James. "I've hurt my wrist."

"Didn't think our fruit cake was that heavy," said the man. "Where's your mother, sonny?"

"She's over there," said Jeremy James, vaguely waving his fruit-cake-holding hand. "With Christopher and Jennifer."

"Ah," said the man.

"Can you tell me where the fish tank is?" asked Jeremy James.

"What fish tank?" asked the man.

"The one with fish in it," said Jeremy James.

"Anybody seen a fish tank?" the man called out.

"Try the fishiotherapy department," said a white-hatted man.

Meanwhile, the young lady with glasses and the tight pigtail had said goodbye to a fair-haired man with an earring and a limp, and was gazing at the empty red chair on which Jeremy James had been but was no longer sitting.

"Oh!" she said.

She looked up the corridor, looked down the corridor, looked right, looked left, said "Oh!" again, called out "Jeremy James!" a few times, and then stood still and thought. Perhaps the boy had gone back to his mother in the waiting-room.

She hurried to the waiting-room, but there was no sign of Jeremy James. A lady was sitting there with two toddlers, and the grey-haired receptionist confirmed that that was Jeremy James's mother.

The receptionist and the

pigtailed lady whispered to each other.

"Should I tell her?"

"Well, I don't know. Don't want to worry her."

"Supposing we can't find him?"

"He must be somewhere."

"Supposing he's been kidnapped?"

In the end they decided that the pigtailed lady should organise a search, and the receptionist should tell Jeremy James's mother.

Before long, there were nurses, porters, and even patients going round asking if anyone had seen a little boy wearing a smart red pullover and holding his left wrist in his right hand. Quite a lot of people had seen him: a young man with long hair remembered saying hello to him, a black lady with a trolley had given him some fruit cake, the cooks in the kitchen had given him more fruit cake, and a doctor and two nurses and three visitors and four patients had all seen him at different times and in different places. But where was he now? Nobody knew. The only clue was that he'd been asking for the fish tank.

The pigtailed lady knew all about the fish tank, and her hopes leapt like a salmon, but when she got there, her hopes sank like a brick. The fish were there, but Jeremy James wasn't.

Then an old lady said she'd seen a little boy walking hand in hand with a man in overalls, and they'd left the hospital. She couldn't remember what the little boy was wearing, but it *might* have been a red pullover.

At this news the pigtailed lady burst into tears, and a doctor said it was time to send for the police, and the grey-haired receptionist told Mummy not to worry, and messages were sent to every ward and every department, and several porters went out to search the car parks and the gardens.

Meanwhile, Jeremy James had wandered through an open double-door and found himself in a large, bright room. There were colourful pictures on the walls, two tables with toy telephones, a rocking-horse with a little girl on it, a tank with a little boy in it, a doll's house, a slide, and more toys and more children.

"Hello," said a boy the same age and size as Jeremy James.

"Hello," said Jeremy James.

"Would you like to play telephones with me?"

"Yes, please," said Jeremy James. "Only I've got to have an egg-ray when the pigtailed lady comes."

The other boy, whose name was Simon, said he'd just had a sandwich and some fruit cake, and he didn't think he could eat an egg-ray on top of all that.

With all the wandering and fish-hunting and fruit cake-eating, Jeremy James was beginning to feel quite warm, and so very carefully, so as not to hurt his wrist, he took off his red pullover, and put it on the floor under a chair. Then he and Simon sat at the tables with the toy telephones.

At that moment a round-faced smiley nurse poked her head round a door and called out: "Everybody all right?"

A chorus of voices cried: "Yes, thank you, Nurse Baker!"

"Good!" said Nurse Baker, and went back into the ward just as one of the porters entered.

"You 'aven't seen a little boy wearin' a red pullover, 'ave yer?" he asked.

"No," said Nurse Baker.

"I s'pose 'e might be in the playroom," said the porter.

"I've just been in there," said Nurse Baker, "and there's certainly no one in a red pullover."

"Ah well, 'e must be somewhere else," said the porter.

By now the police had arrived, and while Jeremy James was dialling 999 to talk to Simon, Mummy was giving a policeman a detailed description of Jeremy James. Another policeman was talking to the old lady who'd seen the boy with the man in the overalls. Someone else had also seen them, and the boy had been wearing a brown jacket, had

57

swung his left arm, and had called the man Daddy.

"Then maybe he was a different boy," said the old lady.

Jeremy James might well have stayed in the playroom for the rest of the day, and maybe even the night as well, if at that moment Simon's mummy and daddy hadn't happened to come in to see their son. First they said hello to Simon, and then they said hello to his new friend, and when they asked the new friend what his name was, Simon's mummy said:

"Isn't that the little boy they're all looking for?"

"Can't be," said Simon's daddy.

"He's supposed to be wearing a red pullover."

"*I've* got a red pullover," said Jeremy James, and pulled it out from under the chair to show them.

"Then you're the one they're looking for," said Simon's daddy.

There was quite a lot of fuss when Jeremy James was finally taken back to see Mummy and the twins. The rosy-cheeked nurse and the pigtailed lady were in tears, the grey-haired receptionist was smiling, two doctors and two policemen were frowning, Jennifer was laughing, Christopher was crying, and Mummy had a sort of pleased-to-see-you-but-where-have-you-been look on her face.

Jeremy James found it all rather puzzling, and told Mummy about the fish tank and the fruit cake and the toy telephones.

One of the policemen took notes, and murmured as he wrote: "Fish tank . . . fruit cake . . . toy telephones . . . Crime o' the century."

Eventually, the policemen said goodbye, the doctors and nurses went back to work, and Jeremy James walked with his right hand in the hand of the pigtailed lady all the way to the X-ray room.

And when she'd finished taking the X-ray, she held his hand all the way back to the waiting-room.

It turned out that Jeremy James had been right. His wrist wasn't broken. The doctor with the thinning red hair and the now-not-quite-so-twinkling blue eyes said it was just a sprain, and the now-extremely-rosy-cheeked nurse put a bandage on it.

There were more goodbyes, and at last Mummy, Jeremy James and the twins slowly made their way towards the big glass doors that self-opened and self-closed. But before they got there, Jeremy

61

James stopped and looked up at Mummy.

"Mummy," he said.

"What is it, Jeremy James?" asked Mummy.

"Before we leave, please can we see the fish tank?"

"No!" said Mummy.

Jeremy James couldn't understand why Mummy said it so sharply.

When I Lived Down Cuckoo Lane and Lost a Fox Fur, and a Lot More Besides

Jean Wills

"Next Saturday your aunts are coming to tea."

I grinned at Mum, and she smiled at me.

The town aunts were good news. I could dress up in their clothes.

Mum would have a good gossip. And we'd all enjoy a tremendous feast.

I asked if my best friend could come as well.

"As long as you're not noisy."

"Noisy? *US?*"

I went and wrote a message and put it in the cricket post.

SATERDAY ARENTS DRESSING UP

It was our favourite game just then. We'd been mothers. Grandmothers. Queens and princesses. But never aunts. And the town aunts were really fancy dressers.

Next time I looked in the wall

there was another message.

CUMING SAT GOD

I looked up at the sky, and Pat and Mick ran out of the alley and captured me.

"So that's what they do with that wall," Mick said.

The cricket post was a secret no longer.

Pat stopped whistling through his gap. "'Cuming Sat God'?"

"'Cuming' is coming. 'Sat' could be Saturday. And 'God' is good," said Mick. "Amen."

They both turned to me.

"What is happening on Saturday?"

I wouldn't tell them anything. My best friend and I were going to have the town aunts all to ourselves.

On Saturday afternoon we hid behind the wall to wait. We waited and waited.

"Suppose they don't come?" my best friend said.

"They're always late. They have to dress up, go to the shops, and catch the train. And the Number 5 bus. They'll come."

Later on two people turned the corner, one short, one tall.

"It's them!"

"At last." We started out, but my best friend stopped. "You didn't say there'd be dogs."

"What dogs?"

"The ones they're carrying."

"They're furs. I told you. The town aunts are fancy dressers."

"And eaters, you said."

"And eaters too." I pointed to the parcels.

We started to run.

The town aunts opened their arms out wide. They kissed us, called us "dear" and "darling", and gave us their parcels to carry.

We made so much noise walking down Cuckoo Lane that people looked out of their windows to watch. Mrs Thresher came out and leaned on her gate. The town aunts laughed, and swept into our house.

Leaving the parcels on the kitchen table we followed them upstairs.

Mum and Dad's bed was soon covered with coats. Hats. Gloves. Furs. The town aunts kicked off their high-heeled shoes. They patted their hair, and powdered their noses. The room was full of a lovely scent.

Then down we all went to open the parcels.

There were chocolate fingers. Coconut creams. Brandy snaps. An iced cake and walnut whips.

Mum made tea in her best silver pot. The best china stood ready on the best silver tray. There were cucumber sandwiches, sausage rolls, and a Dundee cake, as well as everything else.

We packed our share of the feast in the cake box. When Mum and the aunts were safely shut up we crept back upstairs to the bedroom.

"What shall we do first?" my best friend said. "Eat or dress up?"

"Dress up."

My best friend wasn't sure.

"Then we can have a whopping big feast afterwards. And eat the whole lot in one go."

I put on my tall aunt's mauve silk coat. Her black straw hat. And the high-heeled shoes.

"You do look funny," my best friend said. "Miss Baloni gone barmy."

I didn't want to look like Miss Baloni, but my glamorous, exciting town aunt.

My best friend disappeared inside my short aunt's coat. She pulled on a hat like a chimney pot.

"*You* look like Green Hill."

My best friend snatched up a chocolate finger.

"Not yet!"

"Why not?"

And that's when it all went wrong.

As I tottered forward to grab the cake box a cucumber sandwich flew out. My best friend trod on it and fell over. Clutching at the bed she pulled off a fur fox.

"Eurgh! I don't like it. Take it away!"

Instead I wriggled the fox

fur towards her.

She climbed on to the dressing table. I threw the fur, and she threw it back. It hit the window, and flopped on the ledge.

Outside somebody whistled.

"Did you see that?"

"It's not a cat."

"Nor a dog."

"Nor a rabbit."

"It's a fox!"

My best friend climbed down. We crawled beneath the window. I reached up and wriggled the fox. And giggled. And wriggled. And the more I did the more I couldn't stop. And my best friend couldn't either. Until . . .

The fur fell out of the window.

We got tangled up in the town aunts' coats. By the time we looked out Pat and Mick were in the alley, and the fox fur with them.

Downstairs a door opened. Shrieks of laughter blew up the stairs. Then Mum called.

"Are you two still up there?"

"Yes."

"You're not to touch your aunts' things with your sticky fingers."

If only that was all we had done!

"Go out into the garden."

We laid the clothes back on the bed. Took the cake box, and ran downstairs.

Pat and Mick were in the alley, stroking the fox.

"Poor thing," said Mick fiercely. "How would you like it? Glass beads for eyes. Your insides out, and lined with silk."

"It's not my fault," I said.

"We'll bury it. That's what we'll do. Deep in the jungle, where nobody will ever find it." Pat began whistling.

"You can't!" I said.

They walked away.

"I must have it back. I must, I must. I'll give you . . ."

"What?"

They stood at the top of the alley and waited.

I held out the box. ". . . some of this."

They took the whole lot, and ran off with it.

After we'd put the fox fur back we went to see how far Mum and the town aunts had got with their tea. All that talking and laughing . . . There couldn't have been much time for eating.

But . . .

My best friend stared, and so did I. The best china plates were covered in crumbs, nothing else!

As we walked to the bus stop with the town aunts Mrs Thresher leaned on her gate to watch. Windows opened. The fox furs bounced on the town aunts' chests.

"Did you have a lovely feed, my darlings?"

We couldn't speak, just nodded instead. And tried not to think about sausage rolls. Coconut creams. Brandy snaps. Walnut whips. Iced cake. Chocolate fingers. Even a cucumber sandwich would have been something.

As they kissed us goodbye the air was full of their lovely scent. We waved goodbye, then walked back slowly.

"The rotten things," my best friend said. "The greedy, rotten things."

Finding's Keeping

Dorothy Clewes

"It's a find," Shaun said, "– and finding's keeping."

"That's right." Patrick pushed closer to his brother to get a better look. The black wallet looked important – and fat.

Shaun opened it. It bulged with notes – pounds and five-pounds, and with something that looked like a cheque book but wasn't.

"American Traveller's Cheques,"

Shaun read out, very slowly because he had only just learned to read and they were long words – except that the first word was one he knew very well. His eldest sister had gone to live in America. At the time his mother had cried a lot because America was such a long way from Ireland, but now she was glad because Moira was doing so well and was so happy. One day they might all go and join her. But one day didn't mean this year, or next year. It could mean never. It was like the bicycle he had been wanting as long as he could remember: one day, his mother always said, and he still hadn't got one.

"It will belong to a visitor," Patrick said. They came in the spring – like migrating birds, he'd heard his father say – looking for roots. It had given him an instant picture of a land that was bare of grass and trees and flowers, because without roots nothing could grow. He said now to Shaun, "They must have dropped it while they were gathering roots."

Shaun shook his head. He was two years older than Patrick, six, coming up to seven and he knew they weren't the kind of roots Patrick was thinking about. "It's

something to do with family," he
told him, "– like Moira living in
America but her roots are here
in Ireland."

Patrick said, "You mean –
whoever this belonged to might
have lived here, once?"

"That's right. Or their father or
their grandfather." Shaun was
counting the money. "There's
enough to buy a bicycle," he said.
Not a second-hand one which he
would have been delighted with,
but a brand-new one with high
cow-horn handle-bars, and with a
bell, and with side mirrors so that
you could see traffic coming up
from behind.

"Will it buy me a bicycle too?"
Patrick asked.

"You're too little for a proper
bike," Shaun said, "but there'll be
enough left over for a tricycle or a
scooter."

"I'll have a scooter," Patrick said.
On a bicycle you were a long way
off the ground, a scooter was so
low that you could jump off any

moment you liked.

"We'll have to go to Tralee," Shaun said. Tralee was the nearest real town. In their own village of Ballymore there was only one shop which was also a Post Office. You could buy toys there as well as food and stamps, but nothing as big as a bicycle.

Shaun was putting the money back in the wallet after counting it when he saw the airline tickets. He knew at once what they were because they were just like the one Moira had had to buy so that she could fly in an aeroplane all the way to America.

"What's the matter?" Patrick

83

asked him. Shaun was looking as if he had gone suddenly a long way away: not as far as America, but nearly.

"Tickets," Shaun said, "– two of them."

"What good's tickets?" Patrick asked. "They won't buy anything."

"Yes, they will," Shaun said, his voice squeaky with excitement. London/Cork/Shannon/New York, it had said on the tickets – and Moira lived in New York.

"But it's miles and miles away," Patrick reminded him.

"No, it isn't: not in an aeroplane," Shaun said. He was remembering what his father had said to comfort his mother when it was decided that Moira should go to America. "No distance at all," his father had said. "Be there for lunch and back in time for tea. When we have a windfall that's what we'll all do." Well, he and Patrick had got the windfall and that's just what they could do.

"Shannon," Shaun said, "that's where the airport is. It isn't so very far away."

"Too far to walk," Patrick said.

With all that money they ought to have been able to get there by bus, but buses didn't run through Ballymore. "We'll hitch-hike," Shaun said. Boys and girls did it all the time when they came visiting from across the sea. Sometimes big cars stopped for them, and sometimes small cars, and always sooner or later, something stopped.

Shaun stood at the side of the road and waved a hand as he had seen the boys and girls do but nothing stopped for them and after a while they both sat down on the grass by the roadside.

"If we can't get to Shannon we can't use the tickets," Patrick said. He was thinking it would have been much simpler to go into Tralee and buy the bicycle and the scooter – and then there was the

clip-clop of hooves and a voice
they knew called:

"Would you be wanting a lift, at
all?"

It was Mr Murphy with his
donkey cart, taking his milk
churns to the cooperative. The
cooperative was the big factory
where all the milk went to be
bottled. After that it was sent
round to customers in the villages
and towns.

"We have to go to Shannon
Airport," Shaun said, scrambling
up on to the donkey cart and
pulling Patrick up beside him.

"Oh, the airport, is it?"
Mr Murphy said. "It'll be your

87

sister Moira coming home, I'm thinking."

Shaun didn't want to say Yes and he didn't want to say No, so instead he said, "She flew to America from there."

"It's a great day when they come back home," Mr Murphy said. He, too, had a daughter in America, but she hadn't done as well as Moira Rafferty and wouldn't be able to afford to come home for a good bit longer.

They clip-clopped down the dusty road between the hedgerows, Mr Murphy's milk churns making a cheerful clatter. The birds sang high in the sky and the cud-chewing cows lifted up their heads to see who was passing by.

"Isn't it a wonderful thing, now," Mr Murphy said, "that you can be getting to and from across half the world in the time it takes to drive my donkey to the factory and home again?" He shook his head. "The world is shrinking, so it is."

Now they were catching up with other carts taking other milk churns, and now and again there was a little race between the donkeys to see who would get there first – and then in no time at all they were at the factory.

"I'm sorry I can't take you any farther," Mr Murphy said, "but there's Micky O'Connell. He comes from thereabouts. Sit tight now while I have a word with him."

He came back almost at once. "Aren't you the lucky ones?" he said. "Micky will be glad to have you along."

Micky O'Connell worked on a big farm. The farmer had so many cows that the milk they gave filled more than a dozen churns. A donkey cart would have been no use at all so he had to use the farm motor van.

"I don't go all the way to the airport," Micky told them, "but it won't be any trouble for you to get a lift from where I drop you."

After Mr Murphy's donkey cart the motor van seemed to gobble up the road, and the villages, and the towns. Micky dropped them at a crossroads where one of the arms of a sign-post said:

SHANNON AIRPORT 6 MILES

"A great choice of transport you'll have from here," Micky told them, "but mind you don't take just any or your ma'll tan the hide off me." He looked at his watch. "About now Kevin O'Brien comes along on his way to the airport.

You'll know his lorry by the crates of bottles piled high. Tell him you're friends of mine."

A lot of motor cars went whizzing by, most of them full of people and baggage; others were going too fast for their passengers to see anything but the road in front of them – and then a lorry turned the corner.

Shaun and Patrick heard the jingle of its load even before they saw it.

Shaun put out his hand. "Are you Mr Kevin O'Brien?" he asked the young man leaning out of the cab.

"Now how would you be

knowing that?" the young man asked.

Shaun explained.

"Oh – that Micky O'Connell. Sure, any friend of his is a friend of mine," the young man said. "The airport's the very place I'm going to." He got down and gave the boys a leg up into the cab which was so much higher than Mr Murphy's donkey cart and even higher than Micky O'Connell's motor van. "Do you see what I'm carrying?" Kevin said. "Soft drinks. Hundreds and hundreds of bottles in those crates behind, all going to the restaurant at the airport. People get thirsty waiting for aeroplanes."

Patrick was thirsty right now. He said, "When we get to the airport I'll buy one."

"You're going plane-watching," Kevin said. "I used to do that, still do when I get the time."

Shaun said, "We're not going to watch, we're going to fly – to New York."

"Oh yes," Kevin said. "I used to play that game too. Anywhere the planes went, I was on them."

They could see the airport ahead of them now – the terminal building, the runways, the control tower – and a plane just taking off.

"Too bad you missed that one,"

Kevin said, "but there'll be
another taking off in a minute."
He stopped at the terminal
building and they scrambled down.
"Happy landings," he called to
them.

The booking hall was filled with
a great jostle of people. A voice
called over a loud speaker:
"Passengers for New York now
boarding at Gate 6 . . ."

"What's this now?" the man at
the gate said, taking the tickets
Shaun held out to him.

"Two tickets to New York,"
Shaun said.

"So you'll be Mr and Mrs
Regan," the man said.

95

A wave of laughter rippled through the crowd of passengers behind Shaun and Patrick.

"Take them along to the office," the man said to his assistant.

"What will they do to us?" Patrick whispered to Shaun.

Shaun shook his head. He didn't dare to think.

The big man behind the desk looked at them sternly. Ever since Mr Regan had notified them of the loss of his wallet he had been waiting for it to turn up – but not quite like this. He began to quote from the notepad in front of him: "Two tickets to New York, a few traveller's cheques, and £50."

"£52," Shaun said, taking the wallet out of his pocket and putting it on the desk.

"You mean – you didn't spend any of it?" the man asked.

Patrick said, "We were going to buy a bicycle and a scooter—"

". . . and then we saw the tickets and we thought we'd go and see my sister," Shaun finished for him. "She lives in New York."

"Well, what do I do with you?" the man said, and now he was looking even more stern.

You could go to prison for stealing, Shaun was sure of that – and he saw themselves locked up in a dark little room with bars at the window and nothing to eat but bread and water, perhaps for ever, because £52 was a lot of money. He'd been so excited at finding the airline tickets that he hadn't read enough of the writing on the tickets to see that they belonged to someone.

The man was talking again,

reading from the note on his pad:
". . . but it says here: 'If the wallet
is returned the finder is to be
rewarded.'"

Shaun could hardly believe what
the man was saying, but there he
was taking two of the notes out of
the wallet: not one-pound notes,
but five-pound notes. He held them
in his hand, uncertain about
handing them over – and then,
deciding, put them back into the
wallet.

"That's a lot of money for you
two boys to be given when I'm not
sure you deserve it." There was a
long silence and then the man
said, "Well, do you deserve it?" He

glared at them across the desk.

Shaun opened his mouth to answer him but he couldn't make any sound come.

"I'll have your names and address," the man said, pulling a notepad towards him.

They didn't deserve the reward and they weren't going to get it. "Shaun and Patrick Rafferty," Shaun said. "Ballymore." There were only six families in the village, there was no need of a street name.

"Well, Shaun and Patrick Rafferty," the man said – and now Shaun was sure it was going to be the little dark room for them and nothing but bread and water to eat – "the wallet's been returned and the reward has to be handed over. I'll be sending it to your parents and they must decide if you deserve it." And now Shaun thought there was the beginning of a twinkle in the man's eye. "It won't get you to New York to see your sister," he said, "but it might buy a bicycle and a scooter if you're not too choosy. Second-hand was good enough for me when I was your age."

"You mean – you aren't going to lock us up?" Shaun said.

The man shook his head. "Not this time, but in future, remember

– finding is *not* keeping."

"I'm glad we're not going to New York," Patrick said, as they walked from the airport.

"Me, too," Shaun said. "Aeroplanes go too high and too fast. You don't see anything." It couldn't be anything like as good as riding high up in the cab of Kevin O'Brien's lorry, or in Micky O'Connell's farm motor van, or on Mr Murphy's donkey cart – or on a bicycle or a scooter, when they got them.

"Besides, we don't have to go looking for roots," Patrick said, "– they're right here."

House-Mouse

Ursula Moray Williams

Mrs Melody had no children,
no friends, no cat, no dog,
no parrot or budgerigar.
Mrs Melody lived alone.

When people said "Good
morning" to her, she scowled.
When they served her in the shops,
she grumbled. When the postman
brought her letters, she opened
the door the smallest crack to take
them in and banged it shut again.

103

All day long she cleaned her house, wiped the windows, polished the furniture, shone the brasses, and scrubbed the sink. Nobody ever came to see it, which seemed a pity.

Underneath her sink there lived a mouse. He was lonely too. He did no harm in the house. He didn't eat the cheese, he didn't make holes in the wainscot, he didn't leave dirty pawmarks on the shelves. He found all his food out of doors in the garden and only came indoors to get some company.

But Mrs Melody didn't like mice. When she caught sight of him she

shouted and yelled as if a tiger
had come into the kitchen, enough
to frighten any mouse away.

But this mouse did not stay away
for long because he was so lonely.

In the house along the road they
had cats, and dogs, and noisy
children, and terrible mouse traps.

He had very nearly been caught in one. So he came back to Mrs Melody and lived under the sink and tried to keep out of her way.

One day Mrs Melody spent the morning dusting everything in the house, using every one of her four dusters. Afterwards she washed them and hung them out side by side to dry on the clothes line in the garden. Then she emptied out the soapy water, but dropped the soap, and when she stooped to pick it up she slipped and fell headlong, right across the kitchen floor.

She bumped her head on the sink, just where the mouse lived,

106

and out he shot, scared out of his wits, and more scared than ever to find Mrs Melody lying on the floor with her eyes shut.

He ran round and round her. He even tickled her chin with his sharp little nose and whiskers, but nothing would wake her up.

When Mrs Melody did wake up she found she could not move.

"Oh, little mouse! Little mouse! If only you were able to help me!" she said. "If you were a cat you could fetch the neighbours! And if you were a dog you could bark and howl till somebody came. If you were a parrot you could shout: Help! Help! Help! till somebody heard you, but I don't suppose a mouse can do anything at all."

But a mouse could run just as well as a dog or a cat, and at once he ran across the kitchen and out through a crack underneath the door.

He went out into the garden and looked around. On the clothes line Mrs Melody's dusters were blowing in the wind.

Then the mouse had a great idea. He ran up the post that held the line and began to nibble at the dusters. He bit and he bit and he bit, dropping little mouthfuls of cotton to the ground till the first duster looked like a big H. Then he attacked the next, and nibbled it into an E. The third duster became an L and the last a P.

HELP hung on the line, secured by clothes pegs and waving in the wind.

The next-door neighbour saw it from her window.

"Something is wrong at

Mrs Melody's!" she shouted to the lady in the next house, and the lady passed the message down the street. In a minute everybody was running to Mrs Melody's.

The mouse went indoors and retreated underneath the sink. Soon the doctor arrived and then the ambulance. In less than no time Mrs Melody was whisked away to hospital.

Mrs Melody had broken her leg and it took quite a long time to mend. Everyone was kind to her, and the neighbours brought her sweets and fruit and flowers. Mrs Melody began to smile when she saw them coming, and she also smiled at the nurses and the doctors, and even at the other patients. She became quite a popular old lady in the ward.

"But what we can't understand is how you ever hung that message on the clothes line when your leg was broken!" the neighbours said. "If we hadn't seen it, you might be lying there now!"

"What message?" asked Mrs Melody.

They brought her the dusters and laid them out on her bed.

HELP she read.

"It looks almost as if they had been eaten away!" said the neighbours.

"I believe it was my mouse!" said Mrs Melody.

The mouse waited patiently until Mrs Melody came home.

They brought her one day in a taxi, and now all kinds of people came visiting the house.

Mrs Melody was getting on very well indeed.

She had a bright word for all the visitors that came in, and she always introduced them to her mouse.

He felt a little shy now. There was so much unexpected attention. But when the visitors had gone away, and only he and Mrs Melody were left sitting together in the kitchen, he crept out from under the sink and perched on the edge of the grate, washing his whiskers as he listened to her telling him that he was the cleverest mouse in the world, and she meant to keep the dusters for ever to prove it.

The Mermaid Who Pitied a Sailor

Terry Jones

There was once a mermaid who pitied the sailors who drowned in the windy sea.

Her sisters would laugh whenever a ship foundered and sank, and they would swim down to steal the silver combs and golden goblets from the sunken vessels. But Varina, the mermaid, wept in her watery cave, thinking of the men who had lost their lives.

"What in the sea is the matter with you?" her sisters would exclaim. "While we are finding jewels and silver, you sit alone and grieve. It's not our fault if their ships are wrecked! That is the way the sea goes. Besides, these sailors mean nothing to us, sister, for they are not of our kind."

But Varina the mermaid replied, "What though they are not of our kind? Their hopes are still hopes. Their lives are lives."

And her sisters just laughed at

her, and splashed her with their finny tails.

One day, however, a great ship struck the rocks nearby and started to sink. All the other mermaids stayed sitting on the rocks where they had been singing, but Varina slipped away into the sea, and swam around and around the sinking ship, calling out to see if any sailors were still alive.

She saw the Boatswain in his chair, but he had drowned as the ship first took water. She saw the First Mate on the poop deck, but he had drowned, caught in the rigging. She saw the Captain, but he too was lifeless, with his hands around the wheel.

Then she heard a tap-tap-tapping, coming from the side of the sunken ship, and there was the frightened face of the Cabin Boy, peering through a crack.

"How are you still alive, when your ship-mates are all drowned?" asked Varina.

"I'm caught in a pocket of air," replied the Cabin Boy. "But it will not last, and we are now so deep at the bottom of the ocean, that unless I can swim as fast as a fish through the ship's hold, through the galley and up onto the deck,

I shall drown long before I can make my way up to the waves above."

"But I swim faster than forty fishes!" exclaimed the mermaid. And without more ado, she twitched her tail, and swam to the deck, and down through the galley

and along through the ship's hold to the place where the Cabin Boy was trapped in the pocket of air.

Then she took his hand and said, "Hold your landlubberly breath!" And back she swam, faster than forty fishes, back through the ship's hold, back through the galley and up to the deck and then up and up and up to the waves above.

There the Cabin Boy got back his breath. But the moment he turned to the mermaid, it left his body again, for he suddenly saw how beautiful she was.

"Thank you!" he finally managed to say. "Now I can swim to the shore." But the mermaid would not let go of his hand.

"Come with me to my watery cave," she said.

"Oh no!" cried the Cabin Boy. "You have saved my life, and grateful I am more than six times seven, but I know you mermaids are not of our kind and bring us poor sailors only despair."

But still the mermaid would not let go of his hand, and she swam as fast as forty fishes, back to her watery cave.

And there she gave the Cabin Boy sea-kelp and sargassum, bladder-wrack and sea-urchins, all served up on a silver dish. But

the Cabin Boy looked pale as
death and said:

"Your kindness overwhelms me,
and grateful I am more than six
times sixty, but you are not of my
kind, and these ocean foods to me
are thin and savourless. Let me
go."

But the mermaid wrapped him
up in a seaweed bed and said,
"Sleep and tomorrow you may feel
better."

The Cabin Boy replied, "You are
kind beyond words, and grateful
I am more than six times six
hundred, but I am not of your
kind, and this bed is cold and
damp, and my blood runs as chill

121

as seawater in my veins."

Finally the mermaid said to the Cabin Boy, "Shut your eyes, and I shall sing you a song that will make you forget your sorrow."

But at that, the Cabin Boy leapt out of the bed and cried, "Oh no! That you must not! For don't you know it is your mermaids' singing that lulls our senses and lures us poor sailors onto the rocks so that we founder and drown?"

When the mermaid heard this, she was truly astonished. She swam to her sisters and cried out, "Sisters! Throw away those silver combs and throw away those golden goblets that we have stolen from the drowned sailors – for it is our songs that lull these sailors' senses and lure them onto the rocks."

When they heard this, the mermaids all wept salty tears for the lives of the men who had been drowned through their songs. And from that day on the mermaids resolved to sit on the rocks and sing only when they were sure there was no ship in sight.

As for Varina, she swam back to her watery cave, and there she found the Cabin Boy still waiting for her.

"I could not leave," he said

123

taking her hand. "For though we are of different kind, where shall I find such goodness of heart as yours?"

And there and then he took the mermaid in his arms and kissed her, and she wrapped her finny tail around him, and they both fell into the sea.

Then they swam as if they were one creature instead of two – fast as forty fishes – until, at last, they reached the land the Cabin Boy had left, many years before. And there they fell asleep upon the shore – exhausted and sea-worn.

When the Cabin Boy awoke, he

looked and he found Varina still asleep beside him. And as he stared at her, all the breath once again went from his body, for her finny tail had disappeared, and there she lay beside him – no longer a mermaid, but a beautiful girl, who opened her eyes and looked at him not with pity but with love.

Hopscotch

Hannah Cole

Saturday was the best day of
the week. It was the day that
Carole and Angela spent at
Granny and Grandpa's house,
while Mum went to work. Fergus
always went too. Fergus was
Angela's bear.

Granny pulled out the sofa so
that Angela could make a house
behind it for Fergus.

Grandpa put Fergus up in the

plum tree to frighten off the birds that came to eat the buds.

When one of Fergus's legs came off, Grandpa found some very strong thread and Granny sewed the leg back on while Grandpa read a story to take everyone's mind off the operation.

This Saturday, it was raining and raining. It had rained all yesterday and all last night. The sky was dark and the roads were shiny.

"You'd better put Fergus in your bag," said Mum, "if he doesn't want to get soggy on the way there."

The way to Granny and Grandpa's house was along a road

beside the river. There were houses on one side of the road, and water on the other side. The river was not very big, just wide enough for two boats to pass each other without crashing. Not many boats came along the river in winter.

"Why is the river so high up today?" Angela asked. Usually you had to look down to see whether there were any ducks waiting to be fed, but today the water was nearly up to the pavement. It was gushing along, bubbling and swirling. It looked very dark.

"I didn't realise there was such a flood," said Mum.

"It's not a flood," said Carole. "It's just a full river. All this water will go down to the sea, won't it? It always does."

"I hope the river doesn't get any fuller," said Mum, "or it will be over the edge and into the road."

They turned down a road away from the river and into Granny and Grandpa's street. The river was out of sight now. Rainwater was rushing along the gutters at either side of the road and gurgling down the drains. The gutters looked like little streams.

"If the river does overflow," Angela asked, "can't all the water just go down the drains?"

129

"They'll get full up," said Carole.

There were steps up to each front door in Granny and Grandpa's street. Angela ran up them and jumped down again.

"Hurry up," said Carole. "We're getting wet. You don't have to jump off all the steps."

Angela jumped off another set of steps.

"You splashed me," said Carole.

The pavement was so wet that you couldn't jump without making a splash.

"Let's cross the road," said Mum.

"Just let me jump off Sheila's steps," said Angela. Sheila lived opposite Granny and Grandpa's house. Angela ran up her four steps and jumped down. Sheila opened the front door.

"Hello, jumping bean," she said. "How high was the river when you came by?"

Angela put her hand down on the pavement. "Nearly this high," she said.

"That's a bit too high," said Sheila. "I don't know why the Council don't just put it all in bottles and keep it out of mischief."

"Come on!" Carole shouted. "We're crossing over!"

Granny opened her door and waved to Sheila.

"Wretched rain," she said. "Come on in and get your wet things off."

She took off their boots as they stepped in. She always did that. Her floors were very clean. Angela took her coat off and ran to the back window. The garden looked very wet.

Mum didn't come indoors. She was going straight on to work. "I didn't realise the river was so high," she said. "Are you worried about getting flooded?"

"We should be all right even if the roads flood," said Granny. "The water would have to come right up these steps before it reached the front door."

"Listen," Mum said to Carole and Angela. "Granny and Grandpa are going to be worried about the flood. You two must promise to be good."

"I'm always good," said Angela.

"Nobody's *always* good," said Carole. "Specially not you."

Mum set off for work.

Usually Carole and Angela had a second breakfast as soon as they arrived, because their first one had been so rushed. But today Grandpa came downstairs and said, "Two helpers. Good."

"We're taking everything upstairs," Granny said. "Just in case." She disappeared upstairs, carrying the Hoover.

"Just in case what?" Angela asked.

"In case the river gets higher and higher," said Carole, "and great waves come rolling down the road, and the water splashes the door down and fills up the house."

Angela took Fergus out of her rucksack and hugged him.

"Don't worry," said Grandpa. "If the river does get higher, there won't be waves. It will just slop over the edge, and trickle down the road. And if quite a lot of water trickles along here, it might seep under the crack at the bottom of the front door, and make a puddle on the floor. We'd be quite safe upstairs until the water went away again."

That didn't sound so bad.

"Is the rain easing off at all?" Granny asked.

Angela looked out of the window.

"It's still splashing up out of the puddles," she said.

"Let's get everything upstairs," said Granny.

"Everything?" said Angela. The kitchen was full of things. "Even the cupboards?"

"Not the cupboards," said Carole. "They're fixed to the floor."

Granny asked Carole to fill a

cardboard box with the saucepans from the cupboard next to the cooker.

"We don't want them to get muddy if the water does come in," she said.

"The water is very muddy," said Angela. "It was all brown today."

"That's because it's been rushing along, washing away new bits of the riverbank that don't usually get washed. Angela, could you put all the toys in this box?"

Angela opened the toy cupboard in the living room. There were games and puzzles that had been Mum's when she was little, and a few things from when Granny and

Grandpa were children. Carole and Angela played with them when they came to visit. Angela began to take them all out.

"I've found the circus puzzle!" she shouted. "I thought it was lost!"

Carole came in from the kitchen. "We're not doing puzzles now," she whispered. "We're helping Granny and Grandpa."

"I wasn't doing it," said Angela. "Only finding it."

She put all the puzzles at the bottom of the box. There was a little green tin at the back of the cupboard that she had never noticed before. The lid was stuck.

"What's this?" she asked Granny.

"I can't remember," Granny said. "Let's have a look later, when everything is safely upstairs."

Angela filled the box, and put the green tin in last. It rattled. She put Fergus on top, and Grandpa carried the box upstairs.

When she had unloaded the toys upstairs, Angela took Fergus down in the empty box and helped to fill it with books. Grandpa carried the books up, and Granny took up the bookcase, with Fergus lying on the top shelf.

"You shouldn't make Granny and Grandpa carry Fergus up every time," Carole said. "It makes extra work for them."

"That little teddy doesn't weigh a feather," said Grandpa. "He can come for the ride if he wants to."

He gave them other boxes to fill. In the middle of the loading and unloading, they had sandwiches for lunch. Everyone was too busy for real cooking. They looked out and saw that the gutters at the sides of the road were full of dark river-water, not gushing along to gurgle down the drain now, but lying still as a pond, except for the rainwater splattering into them.

"It looks as though the river's come over the bank," said Grandpa.

Granny rolled up the living room carpet. The room looked very bare without it.

"Shall we take the chairs upstairs, Grandpa?" Angela asked.

"You could take that little stool," said Grandpa, "and Carole, could you carry up this lamp, very carefully?"

Angela gave Fergus a ride on the stool, and wondered what was in the green tin.

Grandpa carried the television up.

"I've always wanted to watch it in bed," he said.

The downstairs rooms got emptier and emptier. The rooms

upstairs were so full you could hardly move in them.

When they looked out of the window again, there was no road and no pavement, just water stretching across to Sheila's house. She was standing in her window, looking sadly out at the flood. Angela could see the reflection of Sheila's house upside-down in the water.

Carole and Angela took the tins and packets out of the food cupboard. Angela made a tower of baked bean tins.

"That's not very helpful," said Carole.

"We'd better take the sofa up,"

141

Angela said. "It will get all soggy, like when I spilt my drink on it."

"The stairs aren't wide enough," said Carole.

"The cushions needn't get wet," said Granny. "Could you take one each?"

The sofa looked uncomfortable with no cushions on it.

"Let's stand it up on some bricks," said Grandpa. "That might just be enough to keep it dry, if the water isn't very deep."

Granny fetched some bricks.

"The water's starting to come into the garden," she said.

She and Grandpa held the sofa up off the ground, while Carole pushed a brick under each corner. Then they did the same with the fridge.

"I think that's all we can do for now," Granny said. "We've done well."

Angela took Fergus to the window, to see the flooded road.

"It's stopped raining!" she shouted. "We can bring everything downstairs again!"

"Oh, I am glad it's stopped," said Granny. "But I'm afraid the water won't go down straight away. The river is still rushing along, and the rainwater that fell this morning is still trickling off the land into the river. So we may yet get flooded."

Angela looked out of the back window. The garden was a giant paddling-pool. The plum tree stuck up out of the water.

"Is this house an island?" Angela asked.

"Of course not," said Carole. "It's got houses stuck to it on both sides. Islands have water all round them."

It felt like an island, with water up to the walls, whichever window you looked out of.

Granny leaned out of the kitchen window, and looked at the front door.

"It's up over the bottom step," she said. "Oh dear, I don't want it to come in. It was dreadful last time, with all that mud. We had to scrub it off, and repaint everything. And the smell stayed for weeks. Months. Oh dear."

Angela hugged Granny.

"It won't come in, Granny," she said. "It won't."

"We'd better keep busy," said Granny. "It's no good sitting and watching the water coming up. What shall we do?"

"Let's see what's in that little tin," said Angela.

"Don't bother Granny with little tins," said Carole. "She's much too worried."

"A little tin sounds like a good

idea," said Grandpa. "I wonder what it is? Run and fetch it, Angela."

So Angela ran upstairs for the tin. Granny managed to pull the lid off.

"Chalk," she said.

Angela looked at the sticks of white chalk, none of them quite new. She had hoped for something more interesting.

"What do you use chalk for?" Carole asked.

"Hopscotch, of course," said Granny.

Carole and Angela looked at her.

"Sam," Granny said. "I don't think these children know what

hopscotch is."

"We'd better show them," said Grandpa, "when the garden's dried out. Fancy not knowing what hopscotch is."

"I think we'd better show them right away," said Granny.

"In here?" said Grandpa, looking round at the bare, clean living room floor.

"If the water comes in," Granny said, "it will wash the chalk off, and if the water doesn't come in, I'll be very happy that there's only chalk to clean up."

"I think she's going to draw on the floor," Angela whispered to Carole.

Granny drew a pattern of big squares on the floor, with numbers in them.

"What can we throw?" she asked.

Grandpa fetched a dried bean from the kitchen. Granny stood at one end of the hopscotch pattern, and threw the bean into the square marked number one. Then she jumped across on to the next square, and hopped and jumped to the end of the pattern. She turned round and jumped and hopped back again, and picked up the bean.

"You have to throw it on to the number two square next," she said. "Then three. The throwing gets harder as you go on. And you mustn't step on the lines."

Carole had a turn. Angela wasn't very good at hopping, so Grandpa held her hand. Grandpa had a turn, and hopped on a line.

"You're out!" said Granny.

"Don't make him be out," said Angela. "He's got very big feet."

"All right," said Granny. "One more try."

While they played, Angela had forgotten about the flood. Now she saw Granny looking out of the back window. She looked out too.

"The plum tree has shrunk," Angela said. "It was much taller than that."

"Trees don't shrink," said Carole. "The water has come up, that's all. Whose turn is it?"

Granny was very good at hopscotch. She threw the bean into each square and never missed. She hopped over it, back to it, and picked it up, without ever stepping on a line. Grandpa was good at throwing the bean into the right square. Carole was quite good at it. Angela hardly ever got it into the square that she was aiming at.

"Don't throw it so hard," said Carole, when the bean skidded right across the room.

"Throw it harder," she said, when the bean dropped on to the floor just by Angela's feet.

Angela couldn't get it right. Granny offered to throw the bean for her. Grandpa said she could carry on hopping even if her bean hadn't gone in the right square.

"You can cheat if you like," said Carole kindly, but Angela just sat down and watched the others.

"Where can I draw a special hopscotch for Angela?" said Grandpa.

Granny's big squares had taken up all the middle of the living room floor.

Grandpa took the chalk to the kitchen and drew a smaller set of squares for Angela.

151

"Just up to six," he said. "That's enough for a beginner. Now, I know you're good at throwing the bean into the one square. You practise hard until you can get it into the two and three squares just as well."

He got her a bean from the jar. Angela practised and practised. She found that there was a good way of throwing the bean, rolling it along the floor. She got better at knowing how hard to roll it.

"There's Sheila looking out of her window," said Grandpa. Grandpa opened his front window.

"Isn't it terrible!" he shouted across the flooded road.

"It's still coming up," Sheila called.

"We'll need a boat," Grandpa shouted back. He was joking, but he didn't sound very happy.

He shut the window again, because it was cold.

Granny and Carole had heard the shouting. They came to wave to Sheila, and look out at the water. It felt as though the water was less likely to come right up to the front door if they kept an eye on it. Two of Sheila's front door steps were still above water.

"Move over, Angela," Carole said. "You're squashing me."

153

"Mind Granny's toes," said Grandpa.

"Don't fidget, Angela," said Carole.

Angela went back to her hopscotch. She had got much better at throwing the bean. She decided to try the whole game, all the way up to six. She threw the bean on to one, and hopped to the end and back. She threw it on to two, and hopped to the end and back. She threw it on to three. She kept on throwing and hopping. When she got to six, the bean jumped out of her hand too fast, and went out of the square.

"I nearly did it!" she said. "The

bean just wouldn't go in the six."

"Be quiet," said Carole, by the window. "We're busy worrying about the flood."

Angela tried again. She threw the bean on to one, and on to two, and on to three. She hopped very carefully. When it came to six, she told the bean that it had to go into the six square, and it did. She hopped into one, jumped into two and three, hopped into four, hopped on to five, picked up the bean, turned round and hopped all the way back.

"I did it all the way up to six!" she said.

But no one was listening.

Grandpa had the window open again, and was peering round at their front door steps. "I think the water's gone down a bit," he said.

"It looks just the same to me," said Granny.

"Was it up to that line on the lamp-post before?" Carole asked.

Angela went to look out of the window.

"Don't push," said Carole.

"Mind my toes," said Granny.

"It has gone down," Angela said.

"Do you think so?" said Grandpa.

"You don't really know," said Carole.

"I do," said Angela. "Sheila's got

two and a half steps now. She only had two before."

"I can't bear to watch it," said Granny. "Let's go and have one more game of hopscotch, and then we'll come back and see how Sheila's steps are getting on. She definitely has two and a half now."

They went into the living room and played hopscotch again.

"You're better than me now," Carole told Angela.

When they had all had a turn, they went back to the front window.

"Sheila's got three steps now," said Angela.

Granny opened the window and

peered out at their own steps.

"You're right, Angela," she said. "It really is going down. Thank goodness, we're not going to be flooded this time."

"We'd better celebrate," said Grandpa. "Carole, see if you can find anything nice upstairs."

"I saw some chocolate biscuits," said Carole.

"Good idea," said Grandpa.

Carole fetched the packet of chocolate biscuits from the bedroom.

"There's Sheila," said Granny.

"She'd better have a biscuit too," said Grandpa.

"Can you throw it that far?"

said Angela.

"Granny's the expert at throwing," said Grandpa.

So Granny threw a chocolate biscuit into Sheila's window across the rivery road. It broke in two as she tried to catch it, but she didn't mind.

"We needn't have bothered taking everything upstairs," Sheila called across. "Still, with the downstairs rooms all empty, I suppose we can have a good spring clean."

"Not us," Granny shouted back. "We're busy playing hopscotch."

Round the World with a Tyre

Edward Blishen

When I was not quite five, I lived near a dump. This was a long time ago, and there weren't half the cars on the road that there are now. But on the dump, which was where people threw things away, there were always hundreds of tyres.

My friend Harry Carter and I

loved that dump. We never knew what we'd find. There'd be marvellous tins and beautiful battered boxes. There'd be broken chairs, and tables with only three legs. And there'd be tyres. Every time we went there, we admired the tins and boxes. We tried to make the three-legged tables stand up, which they wouldn't. Then we'd choose a tyre and bowl it away. The bigger the better. I can't remember Harry's face now. That's because it was usually hidden behind the tyre he was bowling down the street.

Sometimes we'd meet another boy bowling *his* tyre in the

opposite direction. And because we were smaller than our tyres, they'd collide and fall over with a great hollow rubbery clunk. And there we'd stand, making angry faces at each other.

"You knocked my tyre over!"

"No, I didn't! *You* knocked *my* tyre over!"

It could lead to battle.

It must have been awkward in those days for any grown-ups who made the mistake of being around. The streets were full of boys bowling enormous tyres! Sometimes, if there was a bit of a slope, we'd lose control. The tyres would roll faster than we could follow them, and if they headed for some unlucky adult, then we'd either have to run after them . . . or just run away.

When the day was over, and I had to go in to bed, I always had the problem of how best to hide my tyre. It had two enemies. One was the boy next door, who wanted it for himself. If I hid it under the hedge at the back of the garden, and my mum called me in at six, and his mum called him in at quarter past six, he had a quarter of an hour to hunt around and find it. Then he'd take it next door and hide it under *his* hedge, and next morning there'd be another battle.

"That's *my* tyre!"

"Prove it!"

I never could. If I said it was a tyre off a motorbike, he'd say his was a tyre off a motorbike too. If I said mine was an extra-big one with DUNLOP written on it, he'd say his was an extra-big one with DUNLOP written on it.

Then I'd lost my tyre.

Its other enemy was my dad or my mum. *He'd* told me hundreds of times that he didn't want to find dirty old tyres under his back hedge. *She'd* said she was tired of washing the dirt off my hands after I'd spent all day bowling those terrible filthy tyres all over the street. And Mrs Grumbler next door had complained that my tyre had only just missed her.

Dirty tyres? Terrible filthy tyres? What a way to talk about tyres! And Mrs Grumbler ought to have told my mum how *clever* I was to miss her. She ought to have said:

"Your lad knows how to control a tyre. You must be proud of him. I've been watching, and he's the best of the lot."

So sometimes I was happy, because I had this particularly fine tyre and it was safely hidden and I could lie in bed and think about bowling it up and down the street all the next day. And sometimes

I was miserable, because my tyre had gone and my mum said I wasn't to go back to the dump and get another one.

"No dump today," she'd say. She'd made me look my best, ready for a visit to Auntie Hilda that afternoon; and look at my face already! "You'd think it had never known what it was to be washed!" I was probably the dirtiest boy there'd ever been in the whole world. "Heaven knows what Auntie Hilda will think!"

But I knew what Auntie Hilda would think. That was because she always said it.

"I give up! Boys are the limit! I

166

think they'd *eat* dirt if you served it up for their dinner!"

If my mum and my aunts had their way, I'd spend my whole life in the bathroom. When one of them was tired of washing me, then another would come and take over.

But I remember one day when all was well. All was wonderfully well!

Harry and I had two of the best tyres we'd ever found on the dump. He had DUNLOP written on his, and on mine I had a pair of wings. It was like an angel without a head. The wings seemed to make this tyre bowl along faster than

167

any I'd ever had before. It was the greatest tyre ever, and of course it was in the hands of the greatest-ever bowler of tyres!

Harry and I set off at a spanking pace in the direction of Africa.

Well, I thought Africa probably wasn't very far beyond the church

at the bottom of the road. I'd gone
past it once or twice with my dad,
but only a step or two. The other
way was the dump, and that was
more or less the end of the world
in that direction. To the left there
was a road we weren't allowed to
go down. To the right there was a
steam laundry. There were great
wheels inside and outside the
building, and immense leather
straps ran round the wheels. The
laundry shook with the movement
of those straps. There was a funnel
on the roof that puffed out steam.
It was as if the laundry was
gasping for breath. It smelt too, of
. . . laundry, and soap, and being

clean. Sometimes I'd think that Mum and Auntie Hilda might take me to the laundry and simply leave me there, to be everlastingly scrubbed and hung up to dry and ironed.

So there we were, Harry and I, that good day, setting off towards Africa. That is, as we thought, down the road to the church. Once there, we'd go twice round the war memorial, and then back home. Mission completed.

And that's where the good day became a bad day.

At some point, unable to see over our tyres, we went wrong. Instead of stopping short at Africa, we headed for the North Pole. That's to say, as I know now, we turned towards the laundry. But we didn't reach it. If we had, we'd have heard all that puffing and known where we were. Instead, we must somehow have turned into a side road.

The tyres were moving beautifully. It was one of those afternoons that go on for ever. We'd never been better than this at tyre bowling. It was definitely the best afternoon of our lives.

But after a time I wondered what had happened to the church.

Harry must have wondered that, too. Because suddenly – he was ahead of me – his tyre began to tremble, and then slowly it fell sideways and then lay flat on the pavement. And I stopped bowling too, and *my* tyre trembled and fell flat on the pavement. And now we could see we weren't anywhere near the church. We weren't even in Africa. We weren't at the North Pole. If there was some terrible name for where we were, it must be Australia. I'd heard of Australia, and it was about as far from home as you could get.

Harry said, "Where are we?"

Well, the houses Harry and I lived in were small and all alike. The houses we were looking at now were big and all different.

I remember one house had a path leading to a front door that had glass over it. You walked up to the front door under glass! I'd never seen anything like it! Our own houses had simple short paths, and simple front doors. Some of the front doors here had great pillars, and little roofs of their own. All *our* houses were known by numbers. I lived in number 232. These houses had names. There wasn't a number to be seen.

Where were we?

Harry said, "What shall we do?"

Mum had said if I was ever lost I was to say I came from 232 East Barnet Road. But who was I to say

173

this to? There was nobody to be
seen.

In *our* streets, there were always
kids, and always quite a few
grown-ups. In *this* street, there
was nobody.

Australia was empty and silent.

I said, "Let's go back the way we
came!"

It was the only idea I had.
Perhaps, if you'd gone wrong, the
thing to do was to turn round and
. . . do what you'd done before, but
backwards.

So Harry and I turned and
picked up our tyres and began
bowling back the way we'd come.
Except, of course, that we weren't

at all sure *which* way we'd come.

I suppose it took ten minutes or so, that return journey. I remember it taking for ever. We just bowled along blindly. This time I was in the lead, and I didn't dare to think of where I was going. I just went. The pavement flew past, grey, grey, grey. All the pavements were the same. Wherever I looked, there was nothing I recognised.

And then . . .

I still remember the joy of it. To think that, after all, I'd see Mum again. And Dad. I'd have my tea, after all. I was even, at that moment, glad to think I'd see

Auntie Hilda again.

At that moment, I WAS GLAD!

Because, to my left, I heard a puffing. I heard the flapping sound the great belts made. I smelt the smell of great cleanliness. I knew where we were.

We'd found the laundry . . .

It wasn't long after that when I went to school for the first time and Miss Stout, our teacher, told us about the world. The world was very big, she said. It was very much bigger than East Barnet. And it was round. There was a man called Christopher Columbus who'd bowled his tyre . . . no, he'd sailed his ship across the huge sea, believing the world was round and he was safe. Lots of people at the time thought that Christopher Columbus would sail off the edge of it and go spinning to his death in space.

But they were wrong, and Christopher Columbus was right. He proved the world was round.

I thought, and I said to Harry, that Christopher Columbus might have been the first to prove it, but Harry and I hadn't been far behind. That afternoon when we couldn't find the church, we'd proved the world was round.

Well, obviously, Harry and I had been round it.

The Thrush Girl

Godfried Bomans

Once upon a time there was a little girl who longed to be able to understand animals. She went to her old grandmother and said, "Oh, Grandmother, I would so love to understand the animals. Can you teach me how to do it?"

The grandmother could do a little magic, but not much.

"Oh, my child," she said, "I can only understand the thrushes, and that is not worth the trouble."

"It is enough for me," replied the little girl. "Please teach me."

So the grandmother taught the little girl to understand the thrushes. It was much easier than she had thought. She had only to be kind to the birds and throw them a few crumbs from time to time.

And when she had learned, she walked through the woods listening to the thrushes. Her grandmother was right. They had not much to say. But the little girl was right, too, because it was enough for her. And she went to her father and said, "Father,

179

bring in the hay, for it will rain tomorrow."

The father believed the child. He brought in the hay and by evening it was stacked in the barn. The next morning it began to rain. All the hay in the district was soaked and only his was dry. The father was glad he had listened to his child, but all the other farmers were angry. They were not pleased about the hay that had been saved; they thought only of their own loss. "That girl is no good," they said, "she will go to the bad."

But the little girl said nothing. She went back to her grandmother and said, "Now I would like to understand the moles as well."

"Oh, my child," replied the grandmother, "what a lot you want. Just be good to the animals, then you will understand them after a time."

It was three months before the little girl could understand the moles too. And one day she said to her father, "Bury the potatoes deep in the ground, for tomorrow it will freeze."

And sure enough, next day it froze. The father had buried his potatoes deep in the ground and they were undamaged. All the other farmers moaned and groaned, for they had not a single

good potato left. He had warned
them all, but they had not listened
to him. They thought the little girl
was bewitched. The little girl said
nothing. Now she wanted to
understand the language of the
bees too. Her grandmother could
not help her, for she herself could
not understand the bees.

"You know more than I now," she
said. "You must learn to talk with
bees in your own way."

So the little girl was very kind to
the bees. She no longer ate honey,
but left what there was in the
hives. And after a little while she
could understand exactly what the
bees were saying to each other.

And one day she went to her
mother and said, "Prop up the
fruit trees in the orchard and lock
the windows tight, for there will
be a great storm tonight."

And that very evening a mighty
wind rose up and devastated all

the houses. The trees bowed and broke and there was great distress in the land. Only the orchard in which the little girl lived stood upright and not a tree was harmed. Other people grew so angry that they said, "The child is bewitched! We will burn her!"

The people came running from every side with dry branches to build a great fire. The little girl stood on top of the pile of branches and called in a loud voice, "Thrushes, thrushes, help me now!"

The people could not understand what she was saying, for it was in bird language, but the thrushes understood her perfectly. And in their thousands they flew down and each plucked a twig from the fire. The little girl was soon standing on the grass and there was no more firewood to be seen. She ran happily home and cried, "Father, Mother, the birds have set me free!"

Oh, how happy they were! But their joy did not last long, for the king's soldiers knocked at the door.

"Open!" they cried. "We have come to fetch the girl!"

She was taken to the market place and there stood a man with a great gleaming axe.

"Your head must come off," he said. "Kneel down and stretch out your neck."

The little girl did as she was told, but as she laid her head on the block she cried in a loud voice, "Bees, bees, help me now!"

The executioner did not understand her, for she spoke in bee language. But the bees understood her perfectly. And just as the executioner raised his axe, there came a loud humming and thousands of bees dived at him with their stings ready to strike. The executioner fell to the ground, dead, and the king's soldiers scattered in terror. The little girl ran home at top speed and cried, "Father, Mother, here I am! The bees have saved me!"

But now the king himself took a hand. He rang the bell and said, "I have come to fetch your daughter. I cannot kill her. But she shall be shut up in a stone tower."

So the girl was taken to a tower with walls fifteen feet thick. The windows had iron bars and the door was shut with three locks. It was so dark that she could see nothing, but she heard the rats and mice scuttling across the stone floor. The little girl sat on the ground and began to weep bitterly.

"I shall never get out," she said.
"Oh, moles, moles, help me now!"

No sooner had she said this than
thousands of moles began to
tunnel under the tower. The walls
began to tilt and topple. The floor
burst open and the bars sprang
out of the window frames. And
suddenly, crash! The tower fell

with a roar that reverberated throughout the country. The king was just having breakfast when he heard it. He put down his knife and fork and said, "The tower has fallen. Did you hear it?"

"Yes, father," said the prince. "Shall I marry her now?"

"I think you should," said the king, "although she is rather small."

And together they stepped into their coach with the four horses and rode at full speed to the house where the little girl lived. She was standing in the garden, scattering crumbs for the birds.

"Will you marry me, later on?"

asked the prince.

"No," said the little girl, "I will not. I do not like the people here. I shall go away."

She packed three jam sandwiches in her basket and added a few blackcurrants. Then she put on her fur-trimmed cloak and went away. And no one ever saw her again.

A Twisty Path

William Mayne

In the long grass beside the big patch of concrete there lived a snail called Levi.

He thought the big patch of concrete might be a road, and there would be somewhere else at the other side. He could not see very far, only about his own length, but there was always something at the end of it.

"I haven't reached the end yet.

I'll keep it in mind," he said.

He pinned a little note up inside his shell, and took another snail's pace through the grass, saying hello to friends like Mr Helix. There was always time for a meal between words.

Now, it was springtime, and moontime, and warm rain time, and the grass was rich and fresh, and, "I should be happy," said Levi to himself.

He ate a green leaf right down to the ground, stalk and all, and it was tender and sweet, but it wasn't what would make him happy.

"Perhaps I need a change," he thought. "I wonder about going to

the other side of the concrete."
But it was very far across, and
he was sure he didn't know the
way.

"What if that's not the going-
across way, but the going-along
way?" he wondered. "I'd never get
anywhere."

He didn't actually know about
places. Snails don't ever move
house, so they don't think about
places. They just change gardens.

Still, Levi wasn't quite happy.
But he went on eating between
words, even when it rained on his
picnic.

When the sun came out he
curled up in his shell and

waited until things were more comfortable.

Sometimes there was something much louder than sunshine, and much nearer. Old Mr Helix, who had the biggest shell of all, said it was lightning.

And sometimes there was a much worse thing, ever so near, and with ever so much smoke and the ground shaking. No one knew what it was, except Levi. "It's frightening," he said. "That's what it is."

"Earthquake," said Mr Helix.

But they hadn't had that for a long time.

One day, when the sun had gone

away, Levi came out and saw what he really needed.

There was the prettiest girl snail anyone could ever hope to see, and she was looking at him. She was looking at him in quite a friendly way. She looked at him as if she might like him, Levi thought.

She had eyes of blue on very elegant stalks. She had a very attractive striped shell. She smiled and showed a charming set of teeth.

Levi fell in love at once. "That's why I'm unhappy," he said to himself. "No one loves me."

"I wonder if it's true," said the girl snail. Her name was Dextry.

They looked at one another. Levi asked whether he could buy her a blade of grass, and she said, "Have one of mine," and they both felt a bit shy.

"But I think it'll be all right," said Levi to himself. "She does like me."

Then Dextry's smile wasn't quite so charming, and her eyes looked at him in a funny way.

"I'm afraid I have to go now," she said, in a sad but certain manner. "I'm afraid we can't be friends."

"But why?" asked Levi. "What is wrong?"

"Simple, I'm afraid," said Dextry. "My shell twists one way, and yours twists the other, and there's nothing we can do about it."

"Shell?" said Levi. "Twists?" And he looked. And she was right. Her shell went one way from the middle, right-handed, and his went the other way, left-handed.

And off Dextry went, quite

slowly, but quite for ever. And Levi
stood where he hoped a bird would
eat him. His heart was broken. He
did not care whether his shell
cracked too.

"Is there a problem?" asked old
Mr Helix, coming by. His shell was
right-handed from the middle too.

"That proves it," said Levi.
"There is something wrong with
me. What shall I do?"

But the sun was coming out and
Mr Helix closed his shell and went
to sleep.

"I shall leave for ever," said Levi.
"But it doesn't feel like Levi for
ever."

In the night he crawled up on the

concrete and set out through the darkness. "Perhaps I'll reach the edge of the world," he said, "and that'll be that."

Well, he was right and he was wrong. He went on until he bumped into something standing there, and climbed up that instead, because it was smooth and easy and cool.

Daylight came, and he found he was up a tower. At least, down was further down than he could see, and up was further up and so were the sides. And it was all white and shining.

He went walking, up and up. "The top will be better," he said, and on he sorrowfully went, weeping a snaily tear now and then from the tips of his eyes, when he thought of Dextry.

Far away down below Dextry was just as unhappy. "But I can't marry a left-twisted snail," she said to herself. "Even if he asks me."

Up on his white tower Levi felt the sun come out. He became very uncomfortable. Tears dried up. His foot began to get hard. His eyes folded right back. He tried to climb into a crack, but it was too small.

Then, all at once, the crack opened up and there was a shadow.

Levi crept through the doorway in the side of a space rocket on its launch pad, while the men set it ready to fire. The men closed the door and went away. Levi was left alone.

Levi climbed up on the flight deck. Levi climbed up on the Control Panel. Levi had a bit of a twirl on the knobs. Levi crawled over the notice that said IGNITION. He thought it just said "Lumpy", because it was. He crawled on to the switch.

"What fun," he thought. "A rocking chair." And he rocked it back.

It was not a rocking chair but a

rocketing switch, and it rocketed. Levi grew a very heavy shell suddenly, and a very flat foot, and his eyes nearly popped out of his head. Mission Control kept shouting to him but not in his language.

All at once he was weightless. He could run, even with only one foot. He could turn somersaults. He could fly.

The only trouble was, he kept coming undone, and had to keep coiling himself up because of the draughtiness in the joints. Even his name came loose and he thought it might be Evil, or Live, or Elvi.

When he felt tidy again he went back to the Control Panel and sat down on RE-ENTRY, to see what happened.

Re-entry happened. The rocket came back to earth. It grew hot, and dizzy, and the right way up, and landed back on its launch pad.

Levi ended up in the corner by the door, hoping his shell was not cracked. When the men came rushing back to see what had gone wrong he rolled out and tumbled to the ground. He landed in the grass, not on the concrete, and went to look for a leaf to eat and shelter under. There was no grass in space.

"Did you find anything interesting?" asked Mr Helix.

"I'm an astrosnail," said Levi. "It was out of this world."

"So I've heard," said Mr Helix. "You missed the earthquake, and there's a friend of yours coming, so I'll be off." And in half a day he was.

And in the same half day Dextry came near him again.

"I wish she wouldn't," said Levi to himself. "My heart is broken. But that's love."

"I'm so sorry," she said. "I really did admire you, and if it wasn't just for one thing, we could be such friends."

"Oh well," said Levi, "that's the way it is," and it was like a dart through his heart.

"Wait a minute," said Dextry. "You've changed. You really have. What have you done?"

"Nothing," said Levi. "Please don't make it worse."

"But you are the right way round now," said Dextry. "We are both the same, and everything will be all right."

"Am I?" said Levi. And he looked. And he was. Somewhere in weightlessness, when he came loose, he had put himself together the other way about, and now they were both the same. Her shell went from the middle, right-handed, and now Levi's went from the middle, right-handed too. "Yes," he said. "I am." He was very surprised, but kept his wits about him. "I did it for you," he said. "Of course."

"Of course," she said. "Now tell me your name."

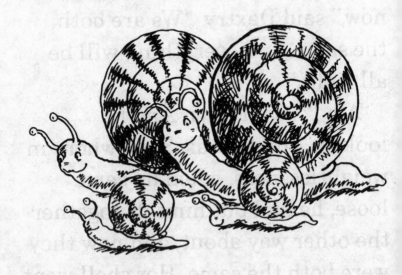

"Ivel," said Levi. Because that had been put the other way round too. "My name is Ivel."

So they lived happily and right-handedly ever afterwards. The children were right-handed, left-handed, and twins.

Josie Smith Gets Lost

Magdalen Nabb

Josie Smith was getting ready to go in the sea. Josie's mum was getting ready too. Josie's gran tied the strings of Josie Smith's bathing costume at the back.

"I'm nearly ready, Mum," said Josie Smith. "Are you nearly ready?"

"Nearly," said Josie's mum.

"The tide's coming right in," said Josie's gran, "so you won't have too far to walk."

"Will it come right up here?" asked Josie Smith.

"Yes," said Josie's gran. "By six o'clock it'll be splashing up against that wall behind us."

"But what about the deck chairs?" asked Josie Smith, "and the donkeys? What about Susie?"

"They'll all be gone," said Josie's gran. "And we'll be gone too."

"Come on," said Josie's mum. "Off we go."

They walked over the soft dry sand and then over the wet hard sand and a patch of shells that hurt their feet. Then tiny waves came racing up to tickle their ankles and run away again.

"It's cold," shouted Josie Smith, hopping up and down.

"We should jump in quickly and get wet all over," said Josie's mum, "then we won't feel it so much."

So they ran as fast as they could through the waves until a bigger wave than all the others came rushing up to them – whoosh – and wet them all over.

"I'm wet all over!" shouted Josie Smith when the wave went away. "Even my hair's wet!"

"It doesn't matter," said Josie's mum. "It'll dry in the sun afterwards."

"Look at the boy with the raft!"

shouted Josie Smith. "And look at the big white duck! Look, Mum! Look at that girl's water wings! Look!"

"I am looking," said Josie's mum.

"Jump me up and down!" shouted Josie Smith.

Josie's mum got hold of her tight and jumped her up and down in the waves.

"Sploosh!" shouted Josie Smith. "Sploosh!" and she closed her eyes as she bounced up and down. Even with her eyes closed she could still see the sparkles that danced on the sea.

"I want to swim!" shouted Josie Smith. "Make me swim!"

Josie's mum turned her over on her tummy and held her tight. Josie Smith kicked and waved as hard as she could.

"Am I swimming?" shouted Josie Smith.

"Nearly," said Josie's mum.

Josie Smith kicked and waved even harder.

"Am I swimming now?" shouted Josie Smith.

"Nearly," said Josie's mum. "Don't try so hard, just enjoy the water. You'll learn in time."

But Josie Smith wanted to learn now, and she went on kicking and waving as hard as she could until she had no breath left.

"I can't swim any more!" shouted Josie Smith.

"Float, then," said Josie's mum. She turned Josie Smith over on her back and held her tight. Josie Smith put her head on the waves and looked at the sky as she bounced slowly up and down. She watched the seagulls flying round and calling and she heard the children in the water all around her, squealing and shouting.

"I like floating," shouted Josie Smith. "I like floating best of all."

"Look out," said Josie's mum, and she lifted Josie Smith up higher.

But she was too late. A big

roaring wave was coming right at them. Blup! Josie Smith's head was under the water. She couldn't see and she couldn't hear anything except the water roaring in her ears. Then it was light again and the children were shouting and splashing but Josie Smith couldn't shout. She couldn't breathe. Everything in her head was stinging and she coughed and choked and choked and coughed and then she heard her mum laughing at her.

"Am I drowning?" shouted Josie Smith as soon as she could breathe again.

"No," said Josie's mum, "but

you're pulling a funny face. You
got a bit of water up your nose,
that's all. It's nice under the water
but you mustn't try and breathe.
Look." And Josie's mum held her
nose and disappeared under the
water so that Josie Smith could
only see her hair floating on top.
"You try."

Josie Smith held her nose and
went under the water and heard
the sea roaring. Then she popped
up and heard the children
shouting.

"You see," said Josie's mum. "It's
good fun."

"Yes," said Josie Smith, but she
didn't like it so very much because

the water was too salty. "Look!"
she shouted. "Look over there!"

A head was bobbing towards
them on the waves. A head with its
nose in the air. Not a girl's head
and not a boy's head and not a
grown-up's head either.

"A big dog!" shouted Josie
Smith. "A big dog, swimming!"

The big dog swam right past
them with his nose in the air and
when he got to the shallow water
he jumped up and shook himself,
wetting all the children who were
paddling there. Then he ran away
along the edge of the sea.

"Come on," said Josie's mum.
"It's time we got out too. We don't

want to get too cold."

They came out where the tiny waves tickled their ankles and ran over the wet hard sand where the shells hurt their feet and then over the soft dry sand to the deck chairs.

Josie's gran was waiting with a big towel.

"Even my hair's wet!" shouted Josie Smith, and she shook her head like the big dog and sprinkled water on her gran's lap. Josie's gran wrapped her up in the big towel that covered even her face and head so that her hair could be rubbed dry. But underneath the towel Josie Smith

went on shouting, though her gran
couldn't hear all the words.

"And we saw a raft –

And a big white duck –

And a girl with water wings –

And swimming –

And floating –

And *drowning* –

And then a big dog came!"

"You'd better get dressed," said
Josie's gran. "You can't sit in a wet
bathing costume in this wind."

Josie Smith got dressed.

"I'll play with my sandcastle
now," she said.

She liked her sandcastle with its
red, white and blue flags flapping
in the wind but she didn't like the

path to it any more because the shells along the edge were broken and sandy.

"Mum," said Josie Smith, "can I go near the sea and collect some good shells in my bucket?"

"All right," said Josie's mum, "but don't be long, and don't go in the water by yourself, even to paddle, in case a wave comes and knocks you down."

"I won't go in the water," said Josie Smith.

"And stay right in front of these deck chairs. Don't wander off or you'll get lost."

"I won't wander off," said Josie Smith. She took her bucket and set off. When she'd gone a little way towards the sea she stopped and turned round to make sure she was going in a straight line and not wandering off.

"My mum's deck chair's red and white striped," she said to herself, "and my gran's deck chair's green and white striped. And there's Eileen's windmill and the big basket in between." She turned round again and kept on going straight towards the sea.

The shells on the wet sand near the water were clean and brightly coloured, pink and blue and brown and white. Some of them were striped and some were shiny inside like pearls. Josie Smith started to fill her bucket. Just when her bucket was half full and she was poking a long dark shell out of the sand with her finger, she heard something come thundering towards her from the sea. Something big and noisy and wet. Something that knocked her down, bump!

It wasn't a wave but it was as wet as a wave and as noisy as a wave and as tall as a wave. It was the big dog who went swimming by himself in the sea.

"Oh!" shouted Josie Smith. "You shouldn't knock people over!"

The big dog shook himself and

showered water all over Josie
Smith.

"Oh!" shouted Josie Smith. "You
shouldn't wet people!"

The big dog sat down with his
tongue hanging out and thumped
his tail on the sand. Josie Smith
sat and looked at him. When they
were both sitting down he was
taller than she was.

"Do you want to play with me?"
she asked him.

The big dog thumped his tail.

"I thought you did," said Josie
Smith, "but you haven't to knock
me over."

The big dog thumped his tail. He
had a collar on with his name on it.

223

"Can I look?" said Josie Smith. She put her face near his collar and he kept his chin up so she could read what was written on it. JIMMIE it said.

"Jimmie," said Josie Smith. "You're called Jimmie."

Jimmie thumped his tail and

licked Josie Smith's face all over.

"Ugh!" said Josie Smith. "You shouldn't lick people's faces, only their hands."

Jimmie jumped up and turned his back on Josie Smith. He started digging with his front paws. Faster and faster he dug until the sand flew up and hit Josie Smith in the face.

"You shouldn't throw sand," shouted Josie Smith. "If it gets in people's eyes, it hurts!"

Jimmie stopped digging and jumped round and round in circles with his front paws pointing.

"Stand still," said Josie Smith, "and we'll play a game. But there's no pushing over, no wetting people and no kicking sand. Right! I'll throw a stick for you."

Josie Smith looked about on the sand until she found a good white stick and then she threw it as far as she could into the water. Jimmie went bounding after it and swam back with it in his mouth. Then he jumped round in circles on the sand, ready to set off again. Josie Smith threw the stick ten times for him and then she said, "I'm tired now, Jimmie."

But Jimmie went on jumping round on the sand, watching for her to throw the stick again. Josie Smith sat down. Jimmie sat down too. He put his head on one side and looked at Josie Smith and then he put his head on the other side and looked at Josie Smith. Then he saw Josie Smith's bucket.

"Woof!" he said, jumping up, and he took the handle of Josie Smith's bucket in his mouth and started running towards the sea.

"My bucket!" shouted Josie Smith, jumping up and running after him. "My bucket! Bring my bucket back! Jimmie!"

But Jimmie was running out to sea with his nose in the air and the bucket handle in his mouth.

All the people in the sea pointed at him and laughed, and when

they heard Josie Smith shouting
they tried to catch Jimmie and get
her bucket for her but Jimmie
turned round and swam away from
them. Josie Smith ran along the
sand to try to keep up with him.
She hadn't to go in the sea by
herself, and anyway, Jimmie was a
long way out where the water was
deep.

"Jimmie!" shouted Josie Smith.
"Jimmie! Come out!"

But Jimmie went swimming
along until, amongst all the
bobbing heads and floating ducks
and water wings, Josie Smith
couldn't see him any more. She
stopped running and sat down on

the sand. Perhaps Jimmie would come back by himself like he came back with the stick. She waited and waited but Jimmie didn't come.

"I'll tell my mum over him," said Josie Smith. She got up and looked back at the deck chairs. They were blue. All of them, as far as Josie Smith could see, were blue. No red and white deck chair, no green and white deck chair, no pink windmill and no basket. The deck chairs were all blue. Josie Smith's chest started thumping, bam-bam-bam, like Jimmie's tail thumping the sand. Then she remembered: she'd run along the sand after Jimmie so

she'd have to run back. She ran a
long way and then stopped to look
at the deck chairs. They were
yellow. No red and white striped
ones, no green and white striped
ones, no pink windmill and no
basket. Josie Smith's chest
thumped harder, bam-bam-bam!
Josie Smith was lost. None of the
other children on the sands were
lost. They were digging and
playing and their mums were
shouting to them and drying them
and giving them things to eat.
Only Josie Smith was lost. Perhaps
she should try running further,
but she didn't know which way.

Then she heard a jingling noise

and saw the donkeys. And the donkey man was nice and he'd tell her where the striped deck chairs were. Josie Smith started running towards the donkeys, her feet thumping the sand and her chest thumping bam-bam-bam. When she got to the donkeys she looked for Susie. Where was Susie? If she saw Susie, everything would be all right. If Susie was there she wasn't really lost.

"Susie," whispered Josie Smith. "Susie . . ." The donkeys nodded and stamped their feet and looked at her but none of them had Susie's friendly face.

They're wearing blue ribbons

now, thought Josie Smith, but they had red and white ribbons before.

She went to the front where the donkey man was bending over a sack of hay.

"Excuse me, Mr Donkey Man," said Josie Smith.

"Too late," said the donkey man. "We're off now." He straightened up and looked at Josie Smith. It wasn't her donkey man at all! It was another man with a cap on and he didn't know Josie Smith. He turned away and started walking off with his donkeys.

"Excuse me! Mr Donkey Man. Excuse me!" Josie Smith trotted after him.

"Too late," said the donkey man again. "We're off."

"I don't want a ride," said Josie Smith, trotting to keep up with him. "I'm looking for a donkey that was here before, called Susie, and there was a man and he didn't have a cap and Susie had red and white ribbons!"

"Susie?" said the donkey man with a cap. "Susie? Red and white ribbons? That'll be Jack Holt's beasts but he's not on this patch. He's further down. No point looking for him now, he'll have gone."

"Why will he have gone?" asked Josie Smith, still trotting.

233

"Tide's coming in," said the donkey man with a cap, and he went off, with all his donkeys following him.

Josie Smith stood still. She looked at the donkeys going away and then she looked at the people in the yellow deck chairs. They were standing up. They were rolling up towels and putting them in bags. The children were putting their shoes and socks on. The grown-ups were folding their deck chairs. They were starting to go away. Something tickled Josie Smith's ankle. She looked down. A little wave had crept up to her feet. It went away again but another one was coming behind it.

"*Tide's coming in*," the donkey man had said.

"*By six o'clock it'll be splashing up against the wall behind us*," Josie's gran had said.

And the deck chairs, and the donkeys . . . ?

"*They'll all be gone*," Josie's gran had said, "*and we'll be gone too*."

Another tiny wave tickled Josie Smith's feet and went away. Josie Smith looked at the sea. It was fierce and glittering, grey and cold and deep, and it was coming nearer.

"*You mustn't try and breathe*," Josie's mum had said. Josie Smith

held her nose and watched the sea.
Could she hold her breath under
the water until the tide went out
again? She remembered the water
roaring in her ears and stinging in
her head and choking her. The
frightening grey sea was coming
nearer, cold and salty, glittering
and deep.

More people were going away.
Josie Smith didn't want to be
lost. She didn't want to drown. She
opened her mouth as far as it
would go and shouted, "Mum!"
And then she began to roar. She
roared so hard that she couldn't
hear anything else and the tears
rolled down her cheeks and into

her mouth, as salty as the sea. She felt somebody put a hand on her head and when she looked through her tears there were people standing all around her. She could see their legs. Bare legs, legs with dresses, legs with trousers, long legs and short legs, fat legs and thin legs. Then a man bent down near Josie Smith's face and said, "What's the matter? Have you hurt yourself?"

"No-o-o!" roared Josie Smith.

"What's the matter, then?" said the man.

"I don't want to dro-own!" roared Josie Smith.

"You're not going to drown," said

237

the man. "Come away from the water. The tide's coming in." And when he said that, Josie Smith roared even louder.

"Perhaps she's lost," a lady said, and she bent down near Josie Smith's face. "Where's your mum?" she asked.

"I don't kno-ow!" roared Josie Smith, "because Jimmie took my bucket away!"

"Who's Jimmie?" asked the lady. "Is he your brother?"

Josie Smith just roared.

"Are your mum and dad on the sands?" asked the lady. "Where are they?"

"Near Susie," roared Josie

Smith. "But Susie's gone!"

"Who's Susie?" asked the lady. "Is she your sister?"

Josie Smith just roared.

"Perhaps she knows where they're staying," the man said. "That might help."

"Do you know where your house is?" asked the lady.

"Across from Mrs Chadwick's shop," roared Josie Smith. "I want my mum!"

"We'll find your mum," the lady said, "if you'll just stop crying and tell me your name, I promise we'll find your mum. That's better. Now then, what's your name?"

"Josie Smith," said Josie Smith.

"Right, you come with me." She got hold of Josie Smith's hand and took her to the steps near the pebbly wall and up to the sandy pavement where the railings went along. Then they climbed a little step into a caravan where a boy was sitting holding a teddy bear and a nice lady was writing in a book at a desk.

"This is Josie Smith," said the lady who was holding her hand. "She got lost on the sands. She's got a brother called Jimmie and a sister called Susie."

"She'll be all right here," said the nice lady who was writing in a book. And the other lady went away.

"Sit down, Josie," said the nice lady, "and tell me what you'd like to play with."

Josie Smith looked around her. There were toys everywhere. She'd never been in a caravan before and she didn't know they were full of toys. Josie Smith looked at them all and then she chose. "The big doll," she said.

The nice lady gave the big doll to Josie Smith. It was nearly as big as she was. Josie Smith sat it on her knee and sniffed its hair. The boy who was holding the teddy bear didn't play with it. He just sat still. Josie Smith sat still too. They were both sitting on stools. Josie Smith looked all around the caravan but she couldn't see any beds to sleep in or any food to eat.

"Where will I go to sleep?" Josie Smith asked the nice lady.

"Are you tired?" the lady asked.

"No," said Josie Smith.

"Do you know where you are?" asked the lady.

"No," said Josie Smith.

"This is the lost children's caravan," the lady said.

"Will I have to live here for ever," asked Josie Smith, "now that I'm a lost child?"

"No," the lady said. "I'm going to make an announcement and your mum will hear it and come for you."

The nice lady pressed a switch and then said in a loud voice, "Will the parents of Josie Smith, the parents of Josie Smith, please come to the lost children's caravan? Will the parents of Josie Smith, the parents of Josie Smith, please come to the lost children's caravan?"

"Can my mum hear you?" asked Josie Smith.

"Yes," said the lady, "everybody on the sands will hear. Your mum will come now, you wait and see."

And as soon as she said it, the door of the caravan opened and

Josie Smith jumped up, ready to go to her mum.

But it wasn't Josie's mum. It was a man, and he took the boy away and the boy cried because they took the teddy bear off him before he went.

Josie Smith sat down again and waited, sniffing the big doll's hair. There was a big lump hurting her throat because nobody came for her. Perhaps her mum and her gran had gone home on the train because the tide had come in. Some tears squeezed out of her eyes but she didn't make a noise. She held the big doll tighter. Then she said in a small voice, "I feel sick."

"Don't worry," the nice lady said. "Your mum will come."

But her mum didn't come.

Josie Smith tried not to cry out loud but it was hard to breathe because of the lump in her throat and she felt cold all over.

"I feel cold," said Josie Smith.

Then she heard a noise at the door. A scratching noise and a thumping noise.

"That's funny," the nice lady said, "perhaps the door's stuck. Maybe this is your mum." She got up and opened the door.

Josie Smith looked but she didn't see her mum.

She saw a bucket. Then she saw a

nose and big ears. And then in came Jimmie, panting and thumping his tail.

"It's Jimmie!" shouted Josie Smith.

"Is it your dog?" asked the nice lady.

"No," said Josie Smith. "But it's my bucket!"

And then in came Josie's mum and Josie's gran.

"Thank goodness we've found you!" said Josie's mum.

"This dog brought us all the way here," said Josie's gran.

And then they said "Thank you" to the nice lady and took Josie Smith away.

When they were on the train going home, Josie Smith snuggled down on the seat between her mum and her gran and said, "Tell me again about Jimmie finding me."

"I've told you three times already," said Josie's mum.

"Tell me again," said Josie Smith.

"Well," said Josie's mum, "first of all we looked up and there was no Josie. Then we walked up and down the sands."

"And no Josie," said Josie Smith.

"And no Josie," said Josie's mum. "And then along came Jimmie and he had a bucket in his mouth that looked like yours."

247

"It *was* mine!" said Josie Smith.

"It was yours," said Josie's mum, "and it still had a few shells in it. And Jimmie jumped round and round in the sand and kept running off and running back, trying to make us follow him, so follow him we did. He took us everywhere you'd been and the people who'd seen you told us you'd been taken to the lost children's caravan, and we thought, where's that?"

"But Jimmie knew," said Josie Smith.

"Jimmie knew," said Josie's mum, "but he ran so fast it was hard to follow him because we

were carrying the big basket and
Eileen's windmill. But he kept
coming back to make sure we were
still there. We were already on our
way to the caravan when we heard
them announce your name."

"But where's Jimmie now?"
asked Josie Smith.

"We don't know," said Josie's
mum. "Once he'd found you
and given you your bucket, he
ran off."

"But he won't stay out in the
dark by himself with no dinner,
will he?" asked Josie Smith.

"No," said Josie's mum, "he'll
have gone home. Dogs don't get
lost."

"And donkeys?" asked Josie Smith.

"Donkeys don't get lost either," said Josie's mum. "Susie will be at home having some dinner too."

"And then what happened?" said Josie Smith. "Tell me."

"And then Jimmie jumped into the caravan," said Josie's mum, "and we went in, too, and we saw you with the big doll on your knee. And then . . ."

But when Josie's mum looked down she saw that Josie Smith's eyes were closed.

Josie Smith was fast asleep. And all the time the train was taking her home she dreamed a long

dream all about Jimmie running
with the bucket in his mouth
beside the glittering silver sea,
and the sand rubbing her legs as
Susie trotted with her big ears
down, and Rosie Margaret and the
lipstick and Eileen's big pink
windmill turning and flapping and
shining in the wind.

The Crooked Little Finger

Philippa Pearce

One morning Judy woke up with a funny feeling in her little finger. It didn't exactly hurt; but it was beginning to ache and it was beginning to itch. It felt wrong. She held it straight out, and it still felt wrong. She curved it in on itself, with all the other fingers, and it still felt wrong.

In the end, she got dressed and went down to breakfast, holding that little finger straight up in the air, quite separately.

She sat down to breakfast, and said to her mother and her father and to her big brother, David, and her young sister, Daisy, "My little finger's gone wrong."

David asked, "What have you done to it?"

"Nothing," said Judy. "I just woke up this morning and it somehow felt wrong."

Her mother said, "I expect you'll wake up tomorrow morning and it'll somehow feel right."

"What about today though?"

asked Judy; but her mother wasn't listening any more.

Her father said, "You haven't broken a bone in your little finger, have you, Judy? Can you bend it? Can you crook it – like this – as though you were beckoning with it?"

"Yes," said Judy; and then: "Ooooow!"

"Did it hurt, then?" said her mother, suddenly listening again, and anxious.

"No," said Judy. "It didn't hurt at all when I crooked it. But it felt *very* funny. It felt wrong. I didn't like it."

David said, "I'm tired of Judy's

little finger," and their mother
said, "Forget your little finger,
Judy, and get on with your
breakfast."

So Judy stopped talking about
her little finger, but she couldn't
forget it. It felt so odd. She tried
crooking it again, and discovered
that it wanted to crook itself. That

was what it had been aching to do
and itching to do.

She crooked it while she poured
milk on her cereal and then
waited for David to finish with the
sugar.

Suddenly –

"Hey!" David cried angrily.
"Don't *do* that, Judy!"

"What is it now?" exclaimed
their mother, startled.

"She snatched the sugar from
under my nose, just when I was
helping myself." He was still
holding the sugar spoon up in the
air.

"I didn't!" said Judy.

"You did!" said David. "How else

did the sugar get from me to you like that?"

"I crooked my little finger at it," said Judy.

David said, "What rubbish!" and their mother said, "Pass the sugar back to David at once, Judy."

Their father said nothing, but stared at Judy's little finger; and Daisy said, "The sugar went quick through the air. I saw it." But nobody paid any attention to Daisy, of course.

Judy began to say, "My little finger—"

But her mother interrupted her. "Judy, we don't want to hear any more at all about that little finger.

There's nothing wrong with it."

So Judy said no more at all about her little finger; but it went on feeling very wrong.

Her father was the first to go, off to work. He kissed his wife goodbye, and his baby daughter, Daisy. He said, "Be a good boy!" to David, and he said, "Be a good girl!" to Judy. Then he stooped and kissed Judy, which he didn't usually do in the morning rush, and he whispered in her ear, "Watch out for that little finger of yours that wants to be crooked!"

Then he went off to work; and, a little later, Judy and David went off to school.

And Judy's little finger still felt wrong, aching and itching in its strange way.

Judy sat in her usual place in the classroom, listening to Mrs Potter reading a story aloud. While she listened, Judy looked around the classroom, and caught sight of an indiarubber she had often seen before and wished was hers. The indiarubber was shaped and coloured just like a perfect little pink pig with a roving eye. It belonged to a boy called Simon, whom she didn't know very well. Even if they had known each other very well indeed, he probably wouldn't have wanted to give Judy his perfect pink pig indiarubber.

As it was, Judy just stared at the indiarubber and longed to have it. While she longed, her little finger began to ache very much indeed and to itch very much indeed. It ached and itched to be allowed to crook itself, to beckon.

In the end Judy crooked her little finger.

Then there was a tiny sound like a puff of breath, and something came sailing through the air from Simon's table to Judy's table, and it landed with a little *flop!* just by Judy's hand. And Mrs Potter had stopped reading the story, and was crying, "What are you doing, Simon Smith, to be throwing indiarubbers about? We don't throw indiarubbers about in this classroom!"

"I didn't throw my indiarubber!" said Simon. He was very much flustered.

"Then how does it happen to be here?" Mrs Potter had come over to Judy's table to pick up the indiarubber. She turned it over, and there was SIMON SMITH written in ink on the under side.

Simon said nothing; and, of course, Judy said nothing; and Mrs Potter said, "We *never* throw indiarubbers about in this classroom, Simon. I shall put this indiarubber up on my desk and there it stays until the dinner-break."

But it didn't stay there – oh, no! Judy waited and waited until no one in the classroom – no one at all – was looking; and then she crooked her little finger, and the indiarubber came sailing through the air again – *flop!* on to her table, just beside her. This time Judy picked it up very quickly and quietly and put it into her pocket.

At the end of the morning, Simon went up to Mrs Potter's desk to get his indiarubber back again; and it wasn't there. He searched round about, and so did Mrs Potter, but they couldn't find the indiarubber. In the end, Mrs Potter was bothered and cross, and Simon was crying. They had no idea where the indiarubber could have got to.

But Judy knew exactly where it was.

Now Judy knew what her little finger could do – what it ached and itched to be allowed to do. But she didn't want anyone else to know what it could do. That would have spoilt everything. She would have had to return Simon's pink pig indiarubber and anything else her little finger crooked itself to get.

So she was very, very careful. At dinner-time she managed to crook her little finger at a second helping of syrup pudding, when no one was looking; and she got it, and ate it. Later on, she crooked her little finger at the prettiest seashell on the Nature table, and no one saw it come through the air to her; and she put it into her pocket with the pink pig indiarubber. Later still, she crooked her finger at another girl's hair-ribbon, that was hanging loose, and at a useful two-coloured pencil. By the end of the school day, the pocket with the pink pig indiarubber was crammed full of things which did not belong to Judy but which had come to her when she crooked her little finger.

And what did Judy feel like? Right in the middle of her – in her stomach – she felt a heaviness, because she had eaten too much syrup pudding.

In her head, at the very top of her head, there was a fizziness of airy excitement that made her feel almost giddy.

And somewhere between the top of her head and her stomach she felt uncomfortable. She wanted to think about all the things hidden in her pocket, and to enjoy the thought; but, on the other hand, she didn't want to think about them at all. Especially she didn't want to think about Simon Smith crying and crying for his pink pig indiarubber. The wanting to think and the *not* wanting to think made her feel very uncomfortable indeed.

When school was over, Judy went home with her brother, David, as usual. They were passing the sweetshop, not far from their home, when Judy said, "I'd like some chocolate, or some toffees."

"You haven't any money to buy chocolate or toffees," said David. "Nor have I. Come on, Judy."

Judy said, "Daisy once went in

there, and the shopman gave her a
toffee. She hadn't any money, and
he *gave* her a toffee."

"That's because she was so little
– a baby, really," said David. "He
wouldn't give you a toffee, if you
hadn't money to buy it."

"It's not fair," said Judy. And her
little finger felt as if it agreed with
her: it ached and it itched, and it
longed to crook itself. But Judy
wouldn't let it – yet. She and David
passed the sweetshop and went on
home to tea.

After tea, it grew dark outside.
Indoors everyone was busy, except
for Judy. Her mother was bathing
Daisy and putting her to bed; her

father was mending something; David was making an aeroplane out of numbered parts. Nobody was noticing Judy, so she slipped out of the house and along the street to the sweetshop.

It was quite dark by now, except for the street-lamps. All the shops were shut; there was nobody about. Judy would have been frightened to be out alone, after dark, without anyone knowing, but her little finger ached and her little finger itched, and she could think of nothing else.

She reached the sweetshop, and looked in through the window. There were pretty tins of toffee and chocolate boxes tied with bright ribbon on display in the window. She peered beyond them, to the back of the shop, where she could just see the bars of chocolate stacked like bricks and the rows of big jars of boiled sweets and the packets and cartons and tubes of sweets and toffees and chocolates and other delightful things that she could only guess at in the dimness of the inside of the shop.

And Judy crooked her little finger.

She held her little finger crooked, and she saw the bars of chocolate and the jars of boiled

sweets and all the other things
beginning to move from the back
of the shop towards the front,
towards the window. Soon the
window was crowded close with
sweets of all kinds pressing
against the glass, as though they
had come to stare at her and at her
crooked little finger. Judy backed
away from the shop window, to the
other side of the street; but she
still held her little finger crooked,
and all the things in the sweetshop
pressed up against the window,
and pressed and crowded and
pressed and pressed, harder and
harder, against the glass of the
shop window, until –

CRACK!

The window shattered, and everything in it came flying out towards Judy as she stood there with her little finger crooked.

She was so frightened that she turned and ran for home as fast as she could, and behind her she heard a hundred thousand things from the sweetshop come skittering and skidding and bumping and thumping along the pavement after her.

She ran and ran and she reached her front gate and then her front door and she ran in through the front door and slammed it shut

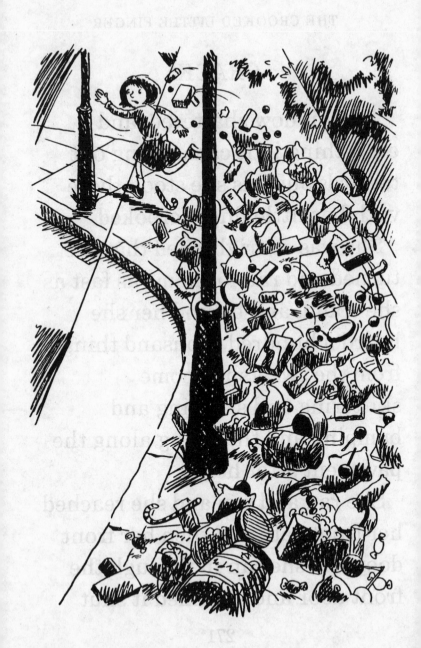

behind her, and heard all the things that had been chasing her come rattling and banging against the front door, and then fall to the ground.

Then she found that she had uncrooked her little finger.

Although she was safe now, Judy ran upstairs to her bedroom and flung herself upon her bed and cried. As she lay there, crying, she held her little finger out straight in front of her, and said to it, "I hate you – I HATE you!"

From her bed, she began to hear shouts and cries and the sound of running feet in the street outside, and her father's voice, and then

her mother's, as they went out to
see what had happened. There
were people talking and talking,
their voices high and loud with
excitement and amazement. Later,
there was the sound of a police car
coming, and more talk.

But, in the end, the noise and the
excitement died away, and at last
everything was quiet. Then she
heard footsteps on the stairs, and
her bedroom door opened, and her
father's voice said, "Are you there,
Judy?"

"Yes."

He came in and sat down on her
bed. He said that her mother was
settling Daisy, so he had come to

tell her what had been happening. He said there had been a smash-and-grab raid at the sweetshop. There must have been a whole gang of raiders, and they had got clean away: no one had seen them. But the gang had had to dump their loot in their hurry to escape. They had thrown it all – chocolates and toffees and sweets and everything – into the first convenient front garden. Judy's father said that the stuff had all been flung into their own front garden and against their own front door.

As she listened, Judy wept and wept. Her father did not ask her why she was crying; but at last he said, "How is that little finger?"

Judy said, "I hate it!"

"I daresay," said her father. "But does it ache and itch any more?"

Judy thought a moment. "No," she said, "it doesn't." She stopped crying.

"Judy," said her father, "if it ever starts aching and itching again, *don't crook it*."

"I won't," said Judy. "I never will again. Never. Ever."

The next day Judy went early to school, even before David. When she got into the classroom, only Mrs Potter was there, at the teacher's desk.

276

Judy went straight to the teacher's desk and brought out from her pocket the pink pig indiarubber and the shell and the hair-ribbon and the two-coloured pencil and all the other things. She put them on Mrs Potter's desk, and Mrs Potter looked at them, and said nothing.

Judy said, "I'm sorry. I'm really and truly sorry. And my father says to tell you that I had a crooked little finger yesterday. But it won't crook itself ever again, ever. I shan't let it."

"I've heard of crooked little fingers," said Mrs Potter. "In the circumstances, Judy, we'll say no more."

And Judy's little finger never crooked itself again, ever.

ACKNOWLEDGEMENTS

The publishers wish to thank the following for permission to reproduce copyright material:

Margaret Stuart Barry: for "The Witch and the Little Village Bus", by permission of the author.

Edward Blishen: for "Round the World with a Tyre" from *A Treasury of Stories for Five Year Olds*, eds. Edward and Nancy Blishen, pp. 35–43. Copyright © Edward Blishen 1989, by permission of Kingfisher Publications Plc.

Godfried Bomans: for "The Thrush Girl" from *The Wily Wizard and the Wicked Witch*, by Godfried Bomans, translated by P. Compton, J M Dent, 1969, by permission of Orion Publishing Group Ltd.

Dorothy Clewes: for "Finding's Keeping", by permission of the author.

Hannah Cole: for "Hopscotch" from *The Best Day of the Week* by Hannah Cole, Walker Books Ltd, 1997, pp. 7–32, by permission of David Higham Associates on behalf of the author.

Anna and Barbara Fienberg: for *Tashi and the Genie*, 1997, by permission of Allen and Unwin Pty Ltd.

Terry Jones: for "The Mermaid Who Pitied a Sailor" from *Fantastic Stories* by Terry Jones, 1992, pp. 31–34, by permission of Pavilion Books.

William Mayne: for "A Twisty Path" from *The Fox Gate and Other Stories* by William Mayne, Hodder Children's Books Ltd, 1996, pp. 37–49, by permission of David Higham Associates on behalf of the author.

Magdalen Nabb: for "Josie Smith Gets Lost" from *Josie Smith At the Seaside* by Magdalen Nabb, William Collins Sons and Co. Ltd, 1989, pp. 63–94, by permission of Harper Collins Publishers Ltd.

Philippa Pearce: for "The Crooked Little Finger" from *The Lion at School and Other Stories* by Philippa Pearce, Viking Kestrel. Copyright © Philippa Pearce 1971, by permission of Laura Cecil Literary Agency on behalf of the author.

Ursula Moray Williams: for "House-Mouse". Copyright © Ursula Moray Williams 1990, by permission of Curtis Brown Ltd, London on behalf of the author.

ACKNOWLEDGEMENTS

Jean Wills: for "When I Lived Down Cuckoo Lane and Lost a Fox Fur, and a Lot More Besides" from *When I Lived Down Cuckoo Lane*, by permission of Anderson Press Ltd.

David Henry Wilson: for "Hospital Fish" from *Do Gerbils Go To Heaven?* by David Henry Wilson, 1996, pp. 7–18, by permission of Macmillan Children's Books.

Every effort has been made to trace the copyright holders but where this has not been possible or where any error has been made the publishers will be pleased to make the necessary arrangement at the first opportunity.

Books in this series available from Macmillan Children's Books

The prices shown below are correct at the time of going to press. However, Macmillan Publishers reserve the right to show new retail prices on covers which may differ from those previously advertised.

All Pan Macmillan titles can be ordered from our website, www.panmacmillan.com, and at your local bookshop or are available by post from:

Bookpost
PO Box 29, Douglas, Isle of Man IM99 1BQ

Credit cards accepted. For details:
Telephone: 01624 836000
Fax: 01624 670923
E-mail: bookshop@enterprise.net
www.bookpost.co.uk

Free postage and packing in the UK.